STAND BY FOR MARS!

Copyright © 2007 BiblioBazaar
All rights reserved
ISBN: 978-1-4346-3204-3

Original copyright: 1952

CAREY ROCKWELL

STAND BY FOR MARS!

A TOM CORBETT SPACE CADET ADVENTURE

STAND BY FOR MARS!

The scarlet-clad figure stood before them

CONTENTS

CHAPTER 1	11
CHAPTER 2	23
CHAPTER 3	34
CHAPTER 4	38
CHAPTER 5	45
CHAPTER 6	52
CHAPTER 7	65
CHAPTER 8	71
CHAPTER 9	77
CHAPTER 10	85
CHAPTER 11	98
CHAPTER 12	108
CHAPTER 13	117
CHAPTER 14	124
CHAPTER 15	131
CHAPTER 16	139
CHAPTER 17	146
CHAPTER 18	153
CHAPTER 19	159
CHAPTER 20	167
CHAPTER 21	174
CHAPTER 22	180

LIST OF ILLUSTRATIONS

The scarlet-clad figure stood before them 6
"I was unable to get a sight on Alpha Centauri" 60
Roger was still standing in front of the Space Queen! 74
"Attention Squadrons D and F—proceed to Luna City" 112
A low muted roar pulsed through the ship 137
"You lead the way, Tom. I'll carry him." 176

CHAPTER 1

"Stand to, you rocket wash!"

A harsh, bull-throated roar thundered over the platform of the monorail station at Space Academy and suddenly the lively chatter and laughter of more than a hundred boys was stilled. Tumbling out of the gleaming monorail cars, they froze to quick attention, their eyes turned to the main exit ramp.

They saw a short, squat, heavily built man, wearing the scarlet uniform of the enlisted Solar Guard, staring down at them, his fists jammed into his hips and his feet spread wide apart. He stood there a moment, his sharp eyes flicking over the silent clusters, then slowly sauntered down the ramp toward them with a strangely light, catfooted tread.

"Form up! Column of fours!"

Almost before the echoes of the thunderous voice died down, the scattered groups of boys had formed themselves into four ragged lines along the platform.

The scarlet-clad figure stood before them, his seamed and weather-beaten face set in stern lines. But there was a glint of laughter in his eyes as he noticed the grotesque and sometimes tortuous positions of some of the boys as they braced themselves in what they considered a military pose.

Every year, for the last ten years, he had met the trains at the monorail station. Every year, he had seen boys in their late teens, gathered from Earth, Mars and Venus, three planets millions of miles apart. They were dressed in many different styles of clothes; the loose flowing robes of the lads from the Martian deserts; the knee-length shorts and high stockings of the boys from the Venusian jungles; the vari-colored jacket and trouser combinations of the boys from the magnificent Earth cities. But they all had one thing in common—a dream. All had visions of becoming Space

Cadets, and later, officers in the Solar Guard. Each dreamed of the day when he would command rocket ships that patrolled the space lanes from the outer edges of Pluto to the twilight zone of Mercury. They were all the same.

"All right now! Let's get squared away!" His voice was a little more friendly now. "My name's McKenny—Mike McKenny. Warrant Officer—Solar Guard. See these hash marks?"

He suddenly held out a thick arm that bulged against the tight red sleeve. From the wrists to the elbow, the lines of boys could see a solid corrugation of white V-shaped stripes.

"Each one of these marks represents four years in space," he continued. "There's ten marks here and I intend making it an even dozen! And no bunch of Earthworms is going to make me lose the chance to get those last two by trying to make a space monkey out of me!"

McKenny sauntered along the line of boys with that same strange catlike step and looked squarely into the eyes of each boy in turn.

"Just to keep the record straight, I'm your cadet supervisor. I handle you until you either wash out and go home, or you finally blast off and become spacemen. If you stub your toe or cut your finger, come to me. If you get homesick, come to me. And if you get into trouble"—he paused momentarily—"don't bother because I'll be looking for *you*, with a fist full of demerits!"

McKenny continued his slow inspection of the ranks, then suddenly stopped short. At the far end of the line, a tall, ruggedly built boy of about eighteen, with curly brown hair and a pleasant, open face, was stirring uncomfortably. He slowly reached down toward his right boot and held it, while he wriggled his foot into it. McKenny quickly strode over and planted himself firmly in front of the boy.

"When I say stand to, I mean stand to!" he roared.

The boy jerked himself erect and snapped to attention.

"I—I'm sorry, sir," he stammered. "But my boot—it was coming off and—"

"I don't care if your pants are falling down, an order's an order!"

The boy gulped and reddened as a nervous titter rippled through the ranks. McKenny spun around and glared. There was immediate silence.

"What's your name?" He turned back to the boy.

"Corbett, sir. Cadet Candidate Tom Corbett," answered the boy.

"Wanta be a spaceman, do ya?" asked Mike, pushing his jaw out another inch.

"Yes, sir!"

"Been studying long hard hours in primary school, eh? Talked your mother and father deaf in the ears to let you come to Space Academy and be a spaceman! You want to feel those rockets bucking in your back out in the stars? *EH?*"

"Yes, sir," replied Tom, wondering how this man he didn't even know could know so much about him.

"*Well, you won't make it* if I ever catch you disobeying orders again!"

McKenny turned quickly to see what effect he had created on the others. The lines of bewildered faces satisfied him that his old trick of using one of the cadets as an example was a success. He turned back to Corbett.

"The only reason I'm not logging you now is because you're not a Space Cadet yet—and won't be, until you've taken the Academy oath!"

"Yes, sir!"

McKenny walked down the line and across the platform to an open teleceiver booth. The ranks were quiet and motionless, and as he made his call, McKenny smiled. Finally, when the tension seemed unbearable, he roared, "At ease!" and closed the door of the booth.

The ranks melted immediately and the boys fell into chattering clusters, their voices low, and they occasionally peered over their shoulders at Corbett as if he had suddenly been stricken with a horrible plague.

Brooding over the seeming ill-fortune that had called McKenny's attention to him at the wrong time, Tom sat down on his suitcase to adjust his boot. He shook his head slowly. He had heard Space Academy was tough, tougher than any other school in the world, but he didn't expect the stern discipline to begin so soon.

"This could be the beginning of the end," drawled a lazy voice in back of Tom, "for some of the more enthusiastic cadets." Someone laughed.

Tom turned to see a boy about his own age, weight and height, with close-cropped blond hair that stood up brushlike all over his head. He was lounging idly against a pillar, luggage piled high around his feet. Tom recognized him immediately as Roger Manning, and his pleasant features twisted into a scowl.

"About what I'd expect from that character," he thought, "after the trick he pulled on Astro, that big fellow from Venus."

Tom's thoughts were of the night before, when the connecting links of transportation from all over the Solar Alliance had deposited the boys in the Central Station at Atom City where they were to board the monorail express for the final lap to Space Academy.

Manning, as Tom remembered it, had taken advantage of the huge Venusian by tricking him into carrying his luggage. Reasoning that since the gravity of Venus was considerably less than that of Earth, he convinced Astro that he needed the extra weight to maintain his balance. It had been a cheap trick, but no one had wanted to challenge the sharpness of Manning's tongue and come to Astro's rescue. Tom had wanted to, but refrained when he saw that Astro didn't mind.

Finishing his conversation on the teleceiver, McKenny stepped out of the booth and faced the boys again.

"All right," he bawled. "They're all set for you at the Academy! Pick up your gear and follow me!" With a quick light step, he hopped on the rolling slidewalk at the edge of the platform and started moving away.

"Hey, Astro!" Roger Manning stopped the huge boy about to step over. "Going to carry my bags?"

The Venusian, a full head taller, hesitated and looked doubtfully at the four suitcases at Roger's feet.

"Come on," prodded Roger in a tone of mock good nature. "The gravity around here is the same as in Atom City. It's the same all over the face of the Earth. Wouldn't want you to just fly away." He snickered and looked around, winking broadly.

Astro still hesitated, "I don't know, Manning. I—uhh—"

"By the rings of Saturn! What's going on here?" Suddenly from outside the ring of boys that had gathered around, McKenny came roaring in, bulling his way to the center of the group to face Roger and Astro.

"I have a strained wrist, sir," began Roger smoothly.

"And this cadet candidate"—he nodded casually toward Astro—"offered to carry my luggage. Now he refuses."

Mike glared at Astro. "Did you agree to carry this man's luggage?"

"Well—I—ah—" fumbled Astro.

"Well? Did you or didn't you?"

"I guess I sorta did, sir," replied Astro, his face turning a slow red.

"I don't hold with anyone doing another man's work, but if a Solar Guard officer, a Space Cadet, or even a cadet candidate gives his word he'll do something, he does it!" McKenny shook a finger in Astro's face, reaching up to do it. "Is that clear?"

"Yes, sir," was the embarrassed reply.

McKenny turned to Manning who stood listening, a faint smile playing on his lips.

"What's your name, Mister?"

"Manning. Roger Manning," he answered easily.

"So you've got a strained wrist, have you?" asked Mike mockingly while sending a sweeping glance from top to bottom of the gaudy colored clothes.

"Yes, sir."

"Can't carry your own luggage, eh?"

"Yes," answered Roger evenly. "I could carry my own luggage. I thought the candidate from Venus might give me a helping hand. Nothing more. I certainly didn't intend for him to become a marked man for a simple gesture of comradeship." He glanced past McKenny toward the other boys and added softly, "And comradeship *is* the spirit of Space Academy, isn't it, sir?"

His face suddenly crimson, McKenny spluttered, searching for a ready answer, then turned away abruptly.

"What are you all standing around for?" he roared. "Get your gear and yourselves over on that slidewalk! Blast!" He turned once again to the rolling platform. Manning smiled at Astro and hopped nimbly onto the slidewalk after McKenny, leaving his luggage in a heap in front of Astro.

"And be careful with that small case, Astro," he called as he drifted away.

"Here, Astro," said Tom. "I'll give you a hand."

"Never mind," replied Astro grimly. "I can carry 'em."

"No, let me help." Tom bent over—then suddenly straightened. "By the way, we haven't introduced ourselves. My name's Corbett—Tom Corbett." He stuck out his hand. Astro hesitated, sizing up the curly-headed boy in front of him, who stood smiling and offering friendship. Finally he pushed out his own hand and smiled back at Tom.

"Astro, but you know that by now."

"That sure was a dirty deal Manning gave you."

"Ah, I don't mind carrying his bags. It's just that I wanted to tell him he's going to have to send it all back. They don't allow a candidate to keep more than a toothbrush at the Academy."

"Guess he'll find out the hard way."

Carrying Manning's luggage as well as their own, they finally stepped on the slidewalk and began the smooth easy ride from the monorail station to the Academy. Both having felt the sharpness of Manning's tongue, and both having been dressed down by Warrant Officer McKenny, they seemed to be linked by a bond of trouble and they stood close together for mutual comfort.

As the slidewalk whisked them silently past the few remaining buildings and credit exchanges that nestled around the monorail station, Tom gave thought to his new life.

Ever since Jon Builker, the space explorer, returning from the first successful flight to a distant galaxy, came through his home town near New Chicago twelve years before, Tom had wanted to be a spaceman. Through high school and the New Chicago Primary Space School where he had taken his first flight above Earth's atmosphere, he had waited for the day when he would pass his entrance exams and be accepted as a cadet candidate in Space Academy. For no reason at all, a lump rose in his throat, as the slidewalk rounded a curve and he saw for the first time, the gleaming white magnificence of the Tower of Galileo. He recognized it immediately from the hundreds of books he had read about the Academy and stared wordlessly.

"Sure is pretty, isn't it?" asked Astro, his voice strangely husky.

"Yeah," breathed Tom in reply. "It sure is." He could only stare at the shimmering tower ahead.

"It's all I've ever wanted to do," said Tom at length. "Just get out there and—be *free*!"

"I know what you mean. It's the greatest feeling in the world."

"You say that as if you've already been up there."

Astro grinned. "Yup. Used to be an enlisted space sailor. Bucked rockets in an old freighter on the Luna City—Venusport run."

"Well, what are you doing here?" Tom was amazed and impressed.

"Simple. I want to be an officer. I want to get into the Solar Guard and handle the power-push in one of those cruisers."

Tom's eyes glowed with renewed admiration for his new friend. "I've been out four or five times but only in jet boats five hundred miles out. Nothing like a jump to Luna City or Venusport."

By now the slidewalk had carried them past the base of the Tower of Galileo to a large building facing the Academy quadrangle and the spell was broken by McKenny's bull-throated roar.

"Haul off, you blasted polliwogs!"

As the boys jumped off the slidewalk, a cadet, dressed in the vivid blue that Tom recognized as the official dress of the Senior Cadet Corps, walked up to McKenny and spoke to him quietly. The warrant officer turned back to the waiting group and gave rapid orders.

"By twos, follow Cadet Herbert inside and he'll assign you to your quarters. Shower, shave if you have to and can find anything to shave, and dress in the uniform that'll be supplied you. Be ready to take the Academy oath at"—he paused and glanced at the senior cadet who held up three fingers—"fifteen hundred hours. That's three o'clock. All clear? Blast off!"

Just as the boys began to move, there was a sudden blasting roar in the distance. The noise expanded and rolled across the hills surrounding Space Academy. It thundered over the grassy quadrangle, vibrating waves of sound one on top of the other, until the very air quivered under the impact.

Mouths open, eyes popping, the cadet candidates stood rooted in their tracks and stared as, in the distance, a long, thin, needlelike ship seemed to balance delicately on a column of flame, then suddenly shoot skyward and disappear.

"Pull in your eyeballs!" McKenny's voice crackled over the receding thunder. "You'll fly one of those firecrackers some day.

But right now you're *Earthworms*, the lowest form of animal life in the Academy!"

As the boys snapped to attention again, Tom thought he caught a faint smile on Cadet Herbert's face as he stood to one side waiting for McKenny to finish his tirade. Suddenly he snapped his back straight, turned sharply and stepped through the wide doors of the building. Quickly the double line of boys followed.

"Did you see that, Astro?" asked Tom excitedly. "That was a Solar Guard patrol ship!"

"Yeah, I know," replied Astro. The big candidate from Venus scratched his chin and eyed Tom bashfully. "Say, Tom—ah, since we sort of know each other, how about us trying to get in the same quarters?"

"O.K. by me, Astro, if we can," said Tom, grinning back at his friend.

The line pressed forward to Cadet Herbert, who was now waiting at the bottom of the slidestairs, a mesh belt that spiraled upward in a narrow well to the upper stories of the building. Speaking into an audioscriber, a machine that transmitted his spoken words into typescript, he repeated the names of the candidates as they passed.

"Cadet Candidate Tom Corbett," announced Tom, and Herbert repeated it into the audioscriber.

"Cadet Candidate Astro!" The big Venusian stepped forward.

"What's the rest of it, Mister?" inquired Herbert.

"That's all. Just Astro."

"No other names?"

"No, sir," replied Astro. "You see—"

"You don't say 'sir' to a senior cadet, Mister. And we're not interested in why you have only one name!" Herbert snapped.

"Yes, sir—uhh—Mister." Astro flushed and joined Tom.

"Cadet Candidate Philip Morgan," announced the next boy.

Herbert repeated the name into the machine, then announced, "Cadet Candidates Tom Corbett, Astro, and Philip Morgan assigned to Section 42-D."

Turning to the three boys, he indicated the spiraling slidestairs. "Forty-second floor. You'll find Section D in the starboard wing."

Astro and Tom immediately began to pile Manning's luggage to one side of the slidestairs.

"Take your luggage with you, Misters!" snapped Herbert.

"It isn't ours," replied Tom.

"Isn't yours?" Herbert glanced over the pile of suitcases and turned back to Tom. "Whose is it then?"

"Belongs to Cadet Candidate Roger Manning," replied Tom.

"What are you doing with it?"

"We were carrying it for him."

"Do we have a candidate in the group who finds it necessary to provide himself with valet service?"

Herbert moved along the line of boys.

"Will Cadet Candidate Roger Manning please step forward?"

Roger slid from behind a group of boys to face the senior cadet's cold stare.

"Roger Manning here," he presented himself smoothly.

"Is that your luggage?" Herbert jerked his thumb over his shoulder.

"It is."

Roger smiled confidently, but Herbert merely stared coldly.

"You have a peculiar attitude for a candidate, Manning."

"Is there a prescribed attitude, Mr. Herbert?" Roger asked, his smile broadening. "If there is, I'll be only too glad to conform to it."

Herbert's face twitched almost imperceptibly. Then he nodded, made a notation on a pad and returned to his post at the head of the gaping line of boys. "From now on, Candidate Manning, you will be responsible for your own belongings."

Tom, Astro, and Philip Morgan stepped on the slidestairs and began their spiraling ascent to the forty-second floor.

"I saw what happened at the monorail station," drawled the third member of Section 42-D, leaning against the bannister of the moving belt. "By the craters of Luna, that Manning felluh sure is a hot operator."

"We found out for ourselves," grunted Astro.

"Say, since we're all bunkin' togethuh, let's get to knowin' each othuh. My name's Phil Morgan, come from Georgia. Where you all from?"

"New Chicago," replied Tom. "Name's Tom Corbett. And this is Astro."

"Hiya." Astro stuck out a big paw and grinned his wide grin. "I guess you heard. Astro's all the name I've got."

"How come?" inquired the Southerner.

"I'm from Venus and it's a custom from way back when Venus was first colonized to just hand out one name."

"Funny custom," drawled Phil.

Astro started to say something and then stopped, clamping his lips together. Tom could see his face turn a slow pink. Phil saw it too, and hastily added:

"Oh—I didn't mean anything. I—ah—" he broke off, embarrassed.

"Forget it, Phil." Astro grinned again.

"Say," interjected Tom. "Look at that!"

They all turned to look at the floor they were passing. Near the edge of the step-off platform on the fourth floor was an oaken panel, inscribed with silver lettering in relief. As they drew even with the plaque, they caught sight of someone behind them. They turned to see Manning, the pile of suitcases in front of him, reading aloud.

" . . . to the brave men who sacrificed their lives in the conquest of space, this Galaxy Hall is dedicated . . ."

"Say, this must be the museum," said Tom. "Here's where they have all the original gear used in the first space hops."

"Absolutely right," said Manning with a smile.

"I wonder if we could get off and take a look?" Astro asked.

"Sure you can," said Roger. "In fact, the Academy regs say every cadet must inspect the exhibits in the space museum within the first week."

The members of Section 42-D looked at Roger questioningly.

"I don't know if we have time." Tom was dubious.

"Sure you have—plenty. I'd hop off and take a look myself but I've got to get this junk ready to ship home." He indicated the pile of bags in front of him.

"Aw, come on, Tom, let's take a look!" urged Astro. "They have the old *Space Queen* in here, the first ship to clear Earth's gravity. Boy, I'd sure like to see her!" Without waiting for the others to agree, the huge candidate stepped off the slidestairs.

"Hey, Astro!" yelled Tom. "Wait! I don't think—" His voice trailed off as the moving stair carried him up to the next floor.

But then a curious thing happened. As other boys came abreast of the museum floor and saw Astro they began to get off and follow him, wandering around gazing at the relics of the past.

Soon nearly half of the cadet candidates were standing in silent awe in front of the battered hull of the *Space Queen*, the first atomic-powered rocket ship allowed on exhibition only fifty years before because of the deadly radioactivity in her hull, created when a lead baffle melted in midspace and flooded the ship with murderous gamma rays.

They stood in front of the spaceship and listened while Astro, in a hushed voice, read the inscription on the bronze tablet.

"—Earth to Luna and return. 7th March 2051. In honor of the brave men of the first atomic-powered spaceship to land successfully on the planet Moon, only to perish on return to Earth..."

"Candidates—staaaaaaaaannnnnd *too*!"

Like a clap of thunder Warrant Officer McKenny's voice jarred the boys out of their silence. He stepped forward like a bantam rooster and faced the startled group of boys.

"I wanna know just *one* thing! Who stepped off that slidestairs *first*?"

The boys all hesitated.

"I guess I was the first, sir," said Astro, stepping forward.

"Oh, you guess you were, eh?" roared McKenny.

Taking a deep breath McKenny launched into a blistering tirade. His choice of words were to be long remembered by the group and repeated to succeeding classes. Storming against the huge Venusian like a pygmy attacking an elephant, McKenny roared, berated and blasted.

Later, when Astro finally reached his quarters and changed into the green coveralls of the cadet candidates, Tom and Phil crowded around him.

"It was Roger, blast him!" said Tom angrily. "He was getting back at you because Cadet Herbert made him carry his own gear."

"I asked for it," grumbled Astro. "Ah, I should've known better. But I just couldn't wait to see the *Queen*." He balled his huge hands into tight knots and stared at the floor.

"Now hear this!!!"

A voice suddenly rasped over the PA system loud-speaker above the door. "All cadet candidates will come to attention to receive the Space Academy oath from Commander Walters." The voice paused. "*AT-TENT-SHUN!* Cadet candidates—Staaaaannnnd *TO!*"

"This is Commander Walters speaking!" A deep, powerful voice purred through the speaker. "The Academy oath is taken individually.

"It is something each candidate locks in his spirit, his mind and his heart. That is why it is taken in your quarters. The oath is not a show of color, it is a way of life. Each candidate will face as closely as possible in the direction of his home and swear by his own individual God as he repeats after me."

Astro stepped quickly to the window port and gazed into the blue heavens, eyes searching out the misty planet Venus. Phil Morgan thought a moment, and faced toward the wall with the inlaid star chart of the sky, thinking of sun-bathed Georgia. Tom Corbett stared straight at a blank wall.

Each boy did not see what was in front of him yet he saw further, perhaps, than he had ever seen before. He looked into a future which held the limitlessness of the universe and new worlds and planets to be lifted out of the oblivion of uncharted depths of space to come.

They repeated slowly . . .

" . . . I solemnly swear to uphold the Constitution of the Solar Alliance, to obey interplanetary law, to protect the liberties of the planets, to safeguard the freedom of space and to uphold the cause of peace throughout the universe . . . to this end, I dedicate my life!"

CHAPTER 2

Tom Corbett's first day at Space Academy began at 0530 hours with the blaring of the *Cadet Corps Song* over the central communicators:

> *"From the rocket fields of the Academy*
> *To the far-flung stars of outer space,*
> *We're Space Cadets training to be*
> *Ready for dangers we may face.*
>
> *Up in the sky, rocketing past*
> *Higher than high, faster than fast,*
> *Out into space, into the sun*
> *Look at her go when we give her the gun.*
>
> *From the rocket fields of the . . ."*

Within sixty seconds, the buildings of the Academy rocked with the impact of three thousand voices singing the last stanza. Lights flashed on in every window. Cadets raced through the halls and across the quadrangle. The central communicator began the incessant mustering of cadets, and the never-ending orders of the day.

" . . . Unit 38-Z report to Captain Edwards for astrogation. Unit 68-E report to Commander Walters for special assignments."

On and on, down the list of senior cadets, watch officers, and the newly arrived Earthworms. Units and individuals to report for training or study in everything from ground assembly of an atomic rocket motor, to the history of the founding of the Solar Alliance, the governing body of the tri-planet civilization.

Tom Corbett stepped out of the shower in Section 42-D and bellowed at the top of his voice.

"Hit the deck, Astro! Make use of the gravity!" He tugged at an outsized foot dangling over the side of an upper bunk.

"Uhhhh-ahhhh-hummmmm," groaned the cadet from Venus and tried to go back to sleep.

Philip Morgan stepped into the shower, turned on the cold water, screeched at the top of his voice, gradually trailing off into countless repetitions of the last verse of the Academy song.

"Damp your tubes, you blasted space monkey," roared Astro, sitting up bleary-eyed.

"What time do we eat?" asked Tom, pulling on the green one-piece coverall of the Earthworm cadet candidates.

"I don't know," replied Astro, opening his mouth in a cavernous yawn. "But it'd better be soon. I like space, but not between my backbone and my stomach!"

Warrant Officer McKenny burst into the room and began to compete with the rest of the noise outside the buildings.

"Five minutes to the dining hall and you'd better not be late! Take the slidestairs down to the twenty-eighth floor. Tell the mess cadet in charge of the hall your unit number and he'll show you to the right table. Remember where it is, because you'll have to find it yourself after that, or not eat. Finish your breakfast and report to the ninety-ninth floor to Dr. Dale at seven hundred hours!"

And as fast as he had arrived, he was gone, a flash of red color with rasping voice trailing behind.

Exactly one hour and ten minutes later, promptly at seven o'clock, the three members of Unit 42-D stood at attention in front of Dr. Joan Dale, along with the rest of the green-clad cadets.

When the catcalls and wolf whistles had died away, Dr. Dale, pretty, trim, and dressed in the gold and black uniform of the Solar Guard, held up her hand and motioned for the cadets to sit down.

"My answer to your—" she paused, smiled and continued, "your enthusiastic welcome is simply—thank you. But we'll have no further repetitions. This is Space Academy—not a primary school!"

Turning abruptly, she stood beside a round desk in the well of an amphitheater, and held up a thin tube about an inch in diameter and twelve inches long.

"We will now begin your classification tests," she said. "You will receive one of these tubes. Inside, you will find four sheets of paper. You are to answer all the questions on each paper and place them back in the tube. Take the tube and drop it in the green outline slot in this wall."

She indicated a four-inch-round hole to her left, outlined with green paint. Beside it, was another slot outlined with red paint. "Remain there until the tube is returned to you in the red slot. Take it back to your desk." She paused and glanced down at her desk.

"Now, there are four possible classifications for a cadet. Control-deck officer, which includes leadership and command. Astrogation officer, which includes radar and communications. And power-deck officer for engine-room operations. The fourth classification is for advanced scientific study here at the Academy. Your papers are studied by an electronic calculator that has proven infallible. You must make at least a passing grade on each of the four classifications."

Dr. Dale looked up at the rows of upturned, unsmiling faces and stepped from the dais, coming to a halt near the first desk.

"I know that all of you here have your hearts set on becoming spacemen, officers in the Solar Guard. Most of you want to be space pilots. But there must be astrogators, radar engineers, communication officers and power-deck operators on each ship, and," she paused, braced her shoulders and added, "some of you will not be accepted for any of these. Some of you will wash out."

Dr. Dale turned her back on the cadets, not wanting to look at the sudden pallor that washed over their faces. It was brutal, she thought, this test. Why bring them all the way to the Academy and then give the tests? Why not start the entrance exams at the beginning with the classification and aptitude? But she knew the answer even before the thoughtful question was completed. Under the fear of being washed out, the weaker ones would not pass. The Solar Guard could not afford to have cadets and later Solar Guard officers who could not function under pressure.

She began handing out the tubes and, one by one, the green-clad candidates stepped to the front of the room to receive them.

"Excuse me, Ma'am," said one cadet falteringly. "If—if—I wash out as a cadet—as a Solar Guard officer cadet"—he gulped several times—"does that mean there isn't any chance of becoming a spaceman?"

"No," she answered kindly. "You can become a member of the enlisted Solar Guard, if you can pass the acceleration tests."

"Thank you, Ma'am," replied the boy and turned away nervously.

Tom Corbett accepted the tube and hurried back to his seat. He knew that this was the last hurdle. He did not know that the papers had been prepared individually, the tests given on the basis of the entrance exams he had taken back at New Chicago Primary Space School.

He opened the tube, pulling out the four sheets, printed on both sides of the paper, and read the heading on the first: ASTROGATION, COMMUNICATIONS, SIGNALS (*Radar*)

He studied the first question.

"... What is the range of the Mark Nine radar-scope, and how far can a spaceship be successfully distinguished from other objects in space? ..."

He read the question four times, then pulled out a pencil and began to write.

Only the rustle of the papers, or the occasional sigh of a cadet over a problem, disturbed the silence in the high-ceilinged room, as the hundred-odd cadets fought the questions.

There was a sudden stir in the room and Tom looked up to see Roger Manning walk to the slot and casually deposit his tube in the green-bordered slot. Then he leaned idly against the wall waiting for it to be returned. As he stood there, he spoke to Dr. Dale, who smiled and replied. There was something about his attitude that made Tom boil. So fast? He glanced at his own papers. He had hardly finished two sheets and thought he was doing fine. He clenched his teeth and bent over the paper again, redoubling his efforts to triangulate a fix on Regulus by using dead reckoning as a basis for his computations.

Suddenly a tall man, wearing the uniform of a Solar Guard officer, appeared in the back of the room. As Dr. Dale looked up and smiled a greeting, he placed his finger on his lips. Steve Strong, Captain in the Solar Guard, gazed around the room at the backs bent over busy pencils. He did not smile, remembering how, only fifteen years before, he had gone through the same torture, racking his brains trying to adjust the measurements of a magnascope prism. He was joined by a thin handsome young man, Lieutenant Judson Saminsky, and finally, Warrant Officer McKenny. They nodded silently in greeting. It would be over soon. Strong glanced at the clock over the desk. Another ten minutes to go.

The line of boys at the slots grew until more than twenty stood there, each waiting patiently, nervously, for his turn to drop the tube in the slot and receive in return the sealed cylinder that held his fate.

Still at his desk, his face wet with sweat, Astro looked at the question in front of him for the fifteenth time.

"... Estimate the time it would take a 300-ton rocket ship with half-filled tanks, cruising at the most economical speed to make a trip from Titan to Venusport. (a) Estimate size and maximum capacity of fuel tanks. (b) Give estimate of speed ship would utilize ..."

He thought. He slumped in his chair. He stared at the ceiling. He chewed his pencil ...

Five seats away, Tom stacked his examination sheets neatly, twisted them into a cylinder and inserted them in the tube. As he passed the line of desks and headed for the slot, a hand caught his arm. Tom turned to see Roger Manning grinning at him.

"Worried, spaceboy?" asked Roger easily. Tom didn't answer. He simply withdrew his arm.

"You know," said Roger, "you're really a nice kid. It's a shame you won't make it. But the rules specifically say 'no cabbageheads.'"

"No talking!" Dr. Dale called sharply from her desk.

Tom walked away and stood in the line at the slots. He found himself wanting to pass more than anything in the world. "Please," he breathed, "please, just let me pass—"

A soft gong began to sound. Dr. Dale stood up.

"Time's up," she announced. "Please put your papers in the tubes and drop them in the slot."

Tom turned to see Astro stuffing his papers in the thin cylinder disgustedly. Phil Morgan came up and stood in back of Tom. His face was flushed.

"Everything O.K., Phil?" inquired Tom.

"Easy as free falling in space," replied the other cadet, his soft Georgian drawl full of confidence. "How about you?"

"I'm just hoping against hope."

The few remaining stragglers hurried up to the line.

"Think Astro'll make it?" asked Phil.

"I don't know," answered Tom, "I saw him sweating over there like a man facing death."

"I guess he is—in a way."

Astro took his place in line and shrugged his shoulders when Tom leaned forward to give him a questioning look.

"Go ahead, Tom," urged Phil. Tom turned and dropped his tube into the green-bordered slot and waited. He stared straight at the wall in front of him, hardly daring to breathe. Presently, the tube was returned in the red slot. He took it, turned it over in his hands and walked slowly back to his desk.

"You're washed out, cabbagehead!" Manning's whisper followed him. "Let's see if you can take it without bawling!"

Tom's face burned and he fought an impulse to answer Manning with a stiff belt in the jaw. But he kept walking, reached his desk and sat down.

Astro, the last to return to his desk, held the tube out in front of him as if it were alive. The room was silent as Dr. Dale rose from her desk.

"All right now, boys," she announced. "Inside the tubes you will find colored slips of paper. Those of you who have red slips will remain here. Those who find green slips will return to their quarters. Blue will go with Captain Strong, orange with Lieutenant Saminsky, and purple with Warrant Officer McKenny. Now—please open the tubes."

There was a tinkling of metal caps and then the slight rustle of paper as each boy withdrew the contents of the tube before him.

Tom took a deep breath and felt inside for the paper. He held his breath and pulled it out. It was green. He didn't know what it meant. He looked around. Phil was signaling to him, holding up a blue slip. Tom's heart skipped a beat. Whatever the colors meant, he and Phil were apart. He quickly turned around and caught Astro's eye. The big Venusian held up a green slip. Tom's heart then nearly stopped beating. Phil, who had breezed through with such confidence, held a blue slip, and Astro, who hadn't even finished the test, held up the same color that he had. It could only mean one thing. Failure. He felt the tears welling in his eyes, but had no strength left to fight them back.

He looked up, his eyes meeting the insolent stare of Roger Manning who was half turned in his seat. Remembering the caustic warning of the confident cadet, Tom fought back the flood in his eyes and glared back.

What would he tell his mother? And his father? And Billy, his brother, five years younger than himself, whom he had promised to bring a flask of water from the Grand Canal on Mars. And his sister! Tom remembered the shining pride in her eyes when she kissed him good-bye at the Stratoport as he left for Atom City.

From the front of the room, McKenny's rasping voice jarred him back to the present.

"Cadets—staaaaaaaand *to*!"

There was a shuffle of feet as the boys rose as one.

"All the purple slips follow me," he roared and turned toward the door. The cadets with purple slips marched after him.

Lieutenant Saminsky stepped briskly to the front of the room.

"Cadets with orange slips will please come with me," he said casually, and another group of cadets left the room.

From the rear of the room Captain Strong snapped out an order.

"Blue slips will come with me!"

He turned smartly and followed the last of Lieutenant Saminsky's cadets out of the room.

Tom looked around. The room was nearly empty now. He looked over at Astro and saw his big friend slumped moodily over against his desk. Then, suddenly, he noticed Roger Manning. The arrogant cadet was not smiling any longer. He was staring straight ahead. Before him on the desk, Tom could see a green slip. So he had failed too, thought Tom grimly. It was poor solace for the misery he felt.

Dr. Dale stepped forward again.

"Will the cadets holding green slips return to their quarters. Those with red slips will remain in their seats," she announced.

Tom found himself moving with difficulty. As he walked through the door, Astro joined him. A look more eloquent than words passed between them and they made their way silently up the slidestairs back to their quarters.

Lying in his bunk, hands under his head, eyes staring into space, Tom asked, "What happens now?"

Sprawled on his bunk, Astro didn't answer right away. He merely gulped and swallowed hard.

"I—I don't know," he finally stammered. "I just don't know."

"What'll you do?"

"It's back to the hold of a Venusport freighter, I guess. I don't know." Astro paused and looked at Tom. "What'll you do?"

"Go home," said Tom simply. "Go home and—and find a job."

"Ever think about the enlisted Solar Guard? Look at McKenny—"

"Yeah—but—"

"I know how you feel," sighed Astro. "Being in the enlisted section—is like—well, being a passenger—almost."

The door was suddenly flung open.

"Haul off them bunks, you blasted Earthworms!"

McKenny stood in the doorway in his usual aggressive pose, and Tom and Astro hit the floor together to stand at attention.

"Where's the other cadet?"

"He went with Captain Strong, sir." answered Tom.

"Oh?" said Mike. And in a surprisingly soft tone he added, "You two pulled green slips, eh?"

"Yes, sir," they replied together.

"Well, I don't know how you did it, but congratulations. You passed the classification tests. Both of you."

Tom just looked at the scarlet-clad, stumpy warrant officer. He couldn't believe his ears. Suddenly he felt as if he had been lifted off his feet. And then he realized that he *was* off his feet. Astro was holding him over his head. Then he dumped him in his bunk as easily as if he had been a child. And at the same time, the big Venusian let out a loud, long, earsplitting yell.

McKenny matched him with his bull-like roar.

"Plug that foghorn, you blasted Earthworm. You'll have the whole Academy in here thinking there's a murder."

By this time Tom was on his feet again, standing in front of McKenny.

"You mean, we made it? We're really in? We're cadets?"

"That's right." McKenny looked at a clip board in his hand and read, "Cadet Corbett, Tom. Qualified for control deck. Cadet Astro. Power deck."

Astro took a deep breath and started another yell, but before he could let go, McKenny clamped a big hand over his mouth.

"You bellow like that again and I'll make meteor dust out of you!"

Astro gulped and then matched Tom's grin with one that spread from ear to ear.

"What happened to Philip Morgan?" asked Tom.

"What color slip did he have?"

"Blue."

"Anything besides green washed out," replied Mike quickly. "Now let's see, you have a replacement for Morgan in this unit. An astrogator."

"Greetings, gentlemen," drawled a voice that Tom recognized without even looking. "Allow me to introduce myself to my new unit-mates. My name is Manning—Roger Manning. But then, we're old friends, aren't we?"

"Stow that rocket wash, Manning," snapped Mike. He glanced at the clock over the door. "You have an hour and forty-five minutes until lunch time. I suggest you take a walk around the Academy and familiarize yourselves with the arrangement of the buildings."

And then, for the first time, Tom saw the hard little spaceman smile.

"I'm glad you made it, boys. All three of you." He paused and looked at each of them in turn. "And I can honestly say I'm looking forward to the day when I can serve under you!"

He snapped his back straight, gave the three startled boys a crisp salute, executed a perfect about-face and marched out of the room.

"And that," drawled Roger, strolling to the bunk nearest the window, "is the corniest bit of space gas I've ever heard."

"Listen, Manning!" growled Astro, spinning around quickly to face him.

"Yeah," purred Roger, his eyes drawn to fine points, hands hanging loosely at his sides. "What would you like me to listen to, Cadet Astro?"

The hulking cadet lunged at Manning, but Tom quickly stepped between them.

"Stow it, both of you!" he shouted. "We're in this room together, so we might as well make the best of it."

"Of course, Corbett—of course," replied Manning easily. He turned his back on Astro, who stood, feet wide apart, neck muscles tight and hands clenched in hamlike fists.

"One of these days I'll break you in two, Manning. I'll close that fast-talking mouth of yours for good!"

Astro's voice was a low growl. Roger stood near the window port and appeared to have forgotten the incident.

The light shining in from the hallway darkened, and Tom turned to see three blue-clad senior cadets arranged in a row just inside the door.

"Congratulations, gentlemen. You're now qualified cadets of Space Academy," said a redheaded lad about twenty-one. "My name is Al Dixon," he turned to his left and right, "and these are cadets Bill Houseman and Rodney Withrop."

"Hiya," replied Tom. "Glad to know you. I'm Tom Corbett. This is Astro—and Roger Manning."

Astro shook hands, the three senior cadets giving a long glance at the size of the hand he offered. Roger came forward smartly and shook hands with a smile.

"We're sorta like a committee," began Dixon. "We've come to sign you up for the Academy sports program."

They made themselves comfortable in the room.

"You have a chance to take part in three sports. Free-fall wrestling, mercuryball and space chess." Dixon glanced at Houseman and Withrop. "From the looks of Cadet Astro, free-fall wrestling should be child's play for him!"

Astro merely grinned.

"Mercuryball is pretty much like the old game of soccer," explained Houseman. "But inside the ball is a smaller ball filled with mercury, making it take crazy dips and turns. You have to be pretty fast even to touch it."

"Sounds like you have to be a little Mercurian yourself," smiled Tom.

"You do," replied Dixon. "Oh, yes, you three play as a unit. Competition starts in a few days. So if you've never played before, you might go down to the gym and start practicing."

"You mentioned space chess," asked Roger. "What's that?"

"It's really nothing more than maneuvers. Space maneuvers," said Dixon. "A glass case, a seven-foot cube, is divided by light shafts into smaller cubes of equal shape and size. Each man has a complete space squadron. Three model rocket cruisers, six destroyers and ten scouts. The ships are filled with gas to make them float, and your power is derived from magnetic force. The problem is to get a combination of cruisers and destroyers and scouts into a space section where it could knock out your opponent's ships."

"You mean," interrupted Astro, "you've got to keep track of all those ships at once?"

"Don't worry, Astro," commented Roger quickly. "You use your muscles to win for dear old 42-D in free-fall wrestling. Corbett here can pound down the grassy field for a goal in mercuryball, and I'll do the brainwork of space chess."

The three visiting cadets exchanged sharp glances.

"Everybody plays together, Manning," said Dixon. "You three take part in each sport as a unit."

"Of course," nodded Roger. "Of course—as a unit."

The three cadets stood up, shook hands all around and left. Tom immediately turned to Manning.

"What was the idea of that crack about brains?"

Manning slouched over to the window port and said over his shoulder, "I don't know how you and your king-sized friend here passed the classifications test, Corbett, and I don't care. But, as you say, we're a unit. So we might as well make adjustments."

He turned to face them with a cold stare.

"I know this Academy like the palm of my hand," he went on. "Never mind how, just take it for granted. *I know it.* I'm here for the ride. For a special reason I wouldn't care to have you know. I'll get my training and then pull out."

He took a step forward, his face a mask of bitterness.

"So from now on, you two guys leave me alone. You bore me to death with your emotional childish allegiance to this—this"—he paused and spit the last out cynically—"space kindergarten!"

CHAPTER 3

"I just can't understand it, Joan," said Captain Steve Strong, tossing the paper on his circular desk. "The psychographs of Corbett, Manning and Astro fit together like gears. And yet—"

The Solar Guard officer suddenly rose and walked over to a huge window that filled the entire north wall of his office, a solid sheet of glass that extended from the high domed ceiling to the translucent flooring. Through the window, he stared down moodily toward the grassy quadrangle, where at the moment several hundred cadets were marching in formation under a hot sun.

"—And yet," continued Strong, "every morning for the last three weeks I've got a report from McKenny about some sort of friction between them!"

"I think it'll work out, Steve," answered the pretty girl in the uniform of the Solar Guard, seated in an easy chair on the other side of the desk.

Joan Dale held the distinction of being the first woman ever admitted into the Solar Guard, in a capacity other than administrative work. Her experiments in atomic fissionables was the subject of a recent scientific symposium held on Mars. Over fifty of the leading scientists of the Solar Alliance had gathered to study her latest theory on hyperdrive, and had unanimously declared her ideas valid. She had been offered the chair as Master of Physics at the Academy as a result, giving her access to the finest laboratory in the tri-planet society.

Now facing the problem of personality adjustment in Unit 42-D, she sat across the desk from her childhood friend, Steve Strong, and frowned.

"What's happened this time?"

"Manning." He paused. "It seems to be all Manning!"

"You mean he's the more aggressive of the three?"

"No—not necessarily. Corbett shows signs of being a number-one spaceman. And that big cadet, Astro"—Strong flashed a white smile that contrasted with his deep space tan—"I don't think he could make a manual mistake on the power deck if he tried. You know, I actually saw him put an auxiliary rocket motor together blindfolded!"

The pretty scientist smiled. "I could have told you that after one look at his classification tests."

"How?"

"On questions concerning the power-deck operations, he was letter perfect—"

"And on the others? Astrogation and control deck?"

"He just skimmed by. But even where the problem involved fuel, power, supply of energy, he offered some very practical answer to the problem." She smiled. "Astro is as much an artist on that power deck as Liddy Tamal doing Juliet in the stereos."

"Yes," mused Strong. "And Corbett is the same on the control deck. Good instinctive intelligence. That boy soaks up knowledge like a sponge."

"Facile mind—quick to grasp the essentials." She smiled again. "Seems to me I remember a few years back when a young lieutenant successfully put down a mutiny in space, and at his promotion to captain, the citation included the fact that he was quick to grasp the essentials."

Strong grinned sheepishly. A routine flight to Titan had misfired into open rebellion by the crew. Using a trick picked up in ancient history books of sea-roving pirates in the seventeenth century, he had joined the mutiny, gained control of the ship, sought out the ring-leaders and restored discipline.

"And Manning," asked Strong. "What about Manning?"

"One of the hardest, brightest minds I've come across in the Academy. He has a brain like a steel trap. He never misses."

"Then, do you think he's acting up because Corbett is the nominal head of the unit? Does he feel that he should be the command cadet in the control deck instead of Corbett?"

"No," replied Dr. Dale. "Not at all. I'm sure he intentionally missed problems about control deck and command in his classification test. He concentrated on astrogation, communications and signal radar. He wanted to be assigned to the radar deck. And he turned in the best paper I've ever read from a cadet to get the post."

Strong threw up his hands. "Then what is it? Here we have a unit, on paper at least, that could be number one. A good combination of brains, experience and knowledge. Everything that's needed. And what is the result? Friction!"

Suddenly a buzzer sounded, and on Steve Strong's desk a small televiewer screen glowed into life. Gradually the stern face of Commander Walters emerged.

"Sorry to disturb you, Steve. Can you spare me a minute?"

"Of course, Commander," replied Strong. "Is anything wrong?"

"Very wrong, Steve. I've been looking over the daily performance reports on Unit 42-D."

"Dr. Dale and I have just been discussing that situation, sir." A relieved expression passed over the commander's face.

"Good! I wanted to get your opinions before I broke up the unit."

"No, sir!" said Strong quickly. "Don't do that!"

"Oh?" replied the commander. On the screen he could be seen settling back in his chair.

"And why not?"

"Well, Joan—er—Dr. Dale and myself feel that the boys of Unit 42-D make it potentially the best in the Academy—if they stay together, sir."

Walters considered this for a moment and then asked thoughtfully, "Give me one good reason why the unit shouldn't be washed out."

"The academy needs boys like this, sir," Steve answered flatly. "Needs their intelligence, their experience. They may be a problem now, but if they're handled right, they'll turn out to be ace spacemen, they'll—"

The commander interrupted. "You're pretty sold on them, aren't you, Steve?"

"Yes, sir, I am."

"You know, tomorrow all the units will be assigned to their personal instructors."

"Yes, sir. And I've selected Lieutenant Wolcheck for this unit. He's tough and smart. I think he's just the man for the job."

"I don't agree, Steve. Wolcheck is a fine officer and with any other unit there'd be no question. But I think we have a better man for the job."

"Whom do you suggest, sir?"

The commander leaned forward in his chair.

"You, Steve."

"Me?"

"What do you think, Joan?"

"I wanted to make the same suggestion, Commander," smiled Joan. "But I didn't know if Steve really would want the assignment."

"Well, what about it, Steve?" asked the commander. "This is no reflection on your present work. But if you're so convinced that 42-D is worth the trouble, then take them over and mold them into spacemen. Otherwise, I'll have to wash them out."

Strong hesitated a moment. "All right, sir. I'll do my best."

On the screen the stern lines in Commander Walters' face relaxed and he smiled approvingly.

"Thanks, Steve," he said softly. "I was hoping you'd say that. Keep me posted."

The screen blacked out abruptly and Captain Strong turned to Joan Dale, a troubled frown wrinkling his brow.

"Huh. I really walked into that one, didn't I?" he muttered.

"It isn't going to be easy, Steve," she replied.

"Easy!" He snorted and walked over to the window to stare blankly at the quadrangle below. "I'd almost rather try a landing on the hot side of Mercury. It would be icy compared to this situation!"

"You can do it, Steve. I know you can." Joan moved to his side to place a reassuring hand on his arm.

The Solar Guard officer didn't answer immediately. He kept on staring at the Academy grounds and buildings spread out before him. When he finally spoke, his voice rang with determination.

"I've got to do it, Joan. I've got to whip those boys into a unit. Not only for their sakes—but for the sake of the Academy!"

CHAPTER 4

The first three weeks of an Earthworm's life at Space Academy are filled with never-ending physical training and conditioning to meet the rigors of rocket flight and life on distant planets. And under the grueling pressure of fourteen-hour days, filled with backbreaking exercises and long forced marches, very few of the boys can find anything more desirable than sleep—and more sleep.

Under this pressure the friction in Unit 42-D became greater and greater. Roger and Astro continually needled each other with insults, and Tom gradually slipped into the role of arbiter.

Returning from a difficult afternoon of endless marching in the hot sun with the prospect of an evening of free-fall wrestling before them, the three cadets dragged themselves wearily onto the slidestairs leading to their quarters, their muscles screaming for rest.

"Another day like this," began Astro listlessly, "and I'm going to melt down to nothing. Doesn't McKenny have a heart?"

"No, just an asteroid," Tom grumbled. "He'll never know how close he came to getting a space boot in the face when he woke us up this morning. Oh, man! Was I tired!"

"Stop complaining, will you?" snarled Roger. "All I've heard from you two space crawlers is gripes and complaints."

"If I wasn't so tired, Roger," said Astro, "I'd give you something to gripe about. A flat lip!"

"Knock it off, Astro," said Tom wearily. The role of keeping them apart was getting tiresome.

"The trouble with you, Astro," pursued Roger, "is that you think with your muscles instead of your head."

"Yeah, I know. And you've got an electronic calculator for a brain. All you have to do is push a button and you get the answers all laid out for you."

They had reached their quarters now and were stripping off their sweat-soaked uniforms in preparation for a cool shower.

"You know, Roger," continued Astro, "you've got a real problem ahead of you."

"Any problem you think I have is no problem at all," was the cool reply.

"Yes, it is," insisted Astro. "When you're ready for your first hop in space, you won't be able to make it!"

"Why not?"

"They don't have a space helmet in the Academy large enough to fit that overinflated head of yours!"

Roger turned slowly and spoke to Tom without looking at him. "Close the door, Corbett!"

"Why?" asked Tom, puzzled.

"Because I don't want any interruptions. I'm going to take that big hunk of Venusian space junk apart."

"Anything you say, you bigmouthed squirt!" roared Astro.

"Hey—knock it off!" yelled Tom, jumping between them and grabbing Astro's arm. "If you guys don't lay off each other, you're going to be thrown out of the Academy, and I'll be thrown out with you! I'll be blasted if I'll suffer for your mistakes!"

"That's a very interesting statement, Corbett!" A deep voice purred from the doorway and the three boys whirled to see Captain Strong walk into the room, his black and gold uniform fitting snugly across the shoulders betraying their latent strength. "Stand to—all of you!"

As the boys quickly snapped to attention, Strong eyed them slowly and then moved casually around the room. He picked up a book, looked out of the window port, pushed a boot to one side and, finally, removed Tom's sweat-stained uniform from a chair and sat down. The cadets held their rigid poses, backs stiff, eyes looking straight ahead.

"Corbett?" snapped Strong.

"Yes, sir?"

"What was the meaning of that little speech I heard a moment ago?"

"I—ah—don't quite understand what you mean, sir," stumbled Tom.

"I think you do," said Strong. "I want to know what provoked you to make such a statement."

"I'd rather not answer that, sir."

"Don't get cute, Corbett!" barked Strong. "I know what's going on in this unit. Were Manning and Astro squaring off to fight?"

"Yes, sir," replied Tom slowly.

"All right. At ease all of you," said Strong. The three boys relaxed and faced the officer.

"Manning, do you want to be a successful cadet here at Space Academy?"

"Yes, sir," answered Roger.

"Then why don't you act like it?" asked Strong.

"Is there something wrong with my work, sir?" Tom recognized the smooth Manning confidence begin to appear, and he wondered if Captain Strong would be taken in.

"Everything's wrong with your work," barked Strong. "You're too smart! Know too much!" He stopped short and then added softly with biting sarcasm, "Why do you know so much, Cadet Manning?"

Roger hesitated. "I've studied very hard. Studied for years to become a Space Cadet," he replied.

"Just to be a cadet or a successful cadet *and* a Solar Guard officer?"

"To be successful at both, sir."

"Tell me, Manning, do you have any ideas on life?"

"That's a pretty general question, sir. Do you mean life as a whole or a specific part of life?" They're fencing with each other, thought Tom. He held his breath as Strong eyed the relaxed, confident cadet.

"A spaceman is supposed to have but one idea in life, Manning. And that idea is *space*!"

"I see, sir," replied Roger, as a faraway look came into his eyes.

"Yes, sir, I have some ideas about life in space."

"I'd like to hear them!" requested Strong coldly.

"Very well, sir." Roger relaxed his shoulders and leaned against the bunk. "I believe space is the last frontier of man—Earthman. It's the last place for man to conquer. It is the greatest adventure of all time and I want to be a part of that adventure."

"Thank you, Manning." Strong's voice was even colder than before. "But as it happens, I can read too. That was a direct quote from the closing paragraph of Jon Builker's book on his trip to the stars!" He paused. "Couldn't you think of anything original to say?"

Roger flushed and gritted his teeth. Tom could hardly keep himself from laughing. Captain Strong had scored heavily!

The Solar Guard officer then turned his attention to Astro.

"Astro, where in the name of the universe did you get the idea you could be an officer in the Solar Guard?"

"I can handle anything with push in it, sir!" Astro smiled his confidence.

"Know anything about hyperdrive?"

"Uhh—no, sir."

"Then you can't handle everything with, as you say, push in it!" snapped Strong.

"Er—no, sir," answered Astro, his face clouding over.

There was a long moment of silence while Strong lifted one knee, swung it over the arm of his chair, and looked steadily at the two half-naked boys in front of him. He smiled lazily.

"Well, for two Earthworms, you've certainly been acting like a couple of space aces!"

He let that soak in while he toyed with the gleaming Academy ring on his finger. He allowed it to flash in the light of the window port, then slipped it off and flipped it over to Corbett.

"Know what that is?" he asked the curly-haired cadet.

"Yes, sir," replied Tom. "Your Academy graduation ring."

"Uh-huh. Now give it to our friend from Venus." Tom gingerly handed Astro the ring.

"Try it on, Astro," invited Strong.

The big cadet tried it on all of his fingers but couldn't get it past the first joint.

"Give it to Manning."

Roger accepted the ring and held it in the palm of his hand. He looked at it with a hard stare, then dropped it in the outstretched hand of the Solar Guard officer. Replacing it on his finger, Strong spoke casually.

"All units design their own rings. There are only three like this in the universe. One is drifting around in space on the finger of Sam Jones. Another is blasting a trail to the stars on the finger of Addy Garcia." He held up his finger. "This is the third one."

Strong got up and began to pace in front of the boys.

"Addy Garcia couldn't speak a word of English when he first came to the Academy. And for eight weeks Sam and I sweated to figure out what he was talking about. I think we spent over a hundred hours in the galley doing KP because Addy kept getting us fouled up. But that didn't bother us because we were a unit. Unit 33-V. Class of 2338."

Strong turned to face the silent cadets.

"Sam Jones was pretty much like you, Astro. Not as big, but with the same love for that power deck. He could always squeeze a few extra pounds of thrust out of those rockets. What he knew about astrogation and control, you could stick on the head of a pin. On long flights he wouldn't even come up to the control deck. He just sat in the power hole singing loud corny songs about the Arkansas mountains to those atomic motors. He was a real power-deck man. But he was a *unit* man first! The only reason I'm here to tell you about it is because he never forgot the unit. He died saving Addy and myself."

The room was still. Down the long hall, the lively chatter of other cadets could be heard as they showered and prepared for dinner. In the distance, the rumble of the slidewalks and test firing of rockets at the spaceport was dim, subdued, powerful.

"The unit is the backbone of the Academy," continued Strong. "It was set up to develop three men to handle a Solar Guard rocket cruiser. Three men who could be taught to think, feel and act as one intelligent brain. Three men who would respect each other and who could depend on each other. Tomorrow you begin your real education. You will be supervised and instructed personally.

"Many men have contributed to the knowledge that will be placed in front of you—brave, intelligent men, who blasted through the atmosphere with a piece of metal under them for a spaceship and a fire in their tail for rockets. But everything they accomplished goes to waste if the unit can't become a single personality. It must be a single personality, or it doesn't exist. The unit is the ultimate of hundreds of years of research and progress. But you have to fight to create it and keep it living. Either you want it, or you get out of the Academy!"

Captain Strong turned away momentarily and Tom and Astro looked at Roger significantly.

"Stand to!"

The three boys snapped to attention as the wide-shouldered captain addressed them again.

"Tomorrow you begin to learn how to think as a single brain. To act with combined intelligence as one person. You either make up your minds to start tomorrow or you report to Commander Walters and resign. There isn't any room here for individuals."

He stepped to the door and paused.

"One more thing. I've been given the job of making you over into spacemen. I'm your unit commander. If you're still here in the morning, I'll accept that as your answer. If you think you can't take"—he paused—"what I'm going to dish out, then you know what you can do. And if you stay, you'll *be* the best unit, or I'll break you in two in the attempt. Unit dis . . . missed!" And he was gone.

The three cadets stood still, not knowing quite what to do or say. Finally Tom stepped before Astro and Roger.

"Well," he said quietly, "how about it, you guys? Are you going to lay off each other now?"

Astro flushed, but Roger eyed Corbett coolly.

"Were you really taken in with that space gas, Tom?" He turned to the shower room. "If you were, then you're more childish than I thought."

"A man died to save another man's life, Roger. Sam Jones. I never knew him. But I've met Captain Strong, and I believe that he would have done the same thing for Jones."

"Very noble," commented Roger from the doorway.

"But I'll tell you this, Manning," said Tom, following him, fighting for self-control, "I wouldn't want to have to depend on you to save my life. And I wouldn't want to be faced with the situation where I would have to sacrifice mine to save yours!"

Roger turned and glared at Tom.

"The Academy regs say that the man on the control deck is the boss of the unit. But I have my private opinion of the man who has that job now!"

"What's that supposed to mean?" asked Tom.

"Just this, spaceboy. There's a gym below where I'll take you *or* your big friend on—together—or one at a time." He paused, a cold smile twisting his lips. "And that offer is good as of right now!"

Tom and Astro looked at each other.

"I'm afraid," began Astro slowly, "that you wouldn't stand much of a chance with me, Manning. So if Tom wants the chore of buttoning your lip, he's welcome to it."

"Thanks, Astro," said Tom evenly. "It'll be my pleasure."

Without another word, the three cadets walked out of the door.

CHAPTER 5

"Will this do, Manning?" asked Tom.

The three boys were in a secluded corner of the gym, a large hall on the fourteenth floor of the dormitory building. At the far end of the gym, a group of cadets had just finished a game of mercuryball and were sauntering to the showers. When the last boy had disappeared, the floor was deserted except for Tom, Roger and Astro.

"This will do fine, Corbett," said Roger.

The boxing ring had been taken down the week before to make room for drills and the physical exercises of the Earthworms, so the three boys had to improvise a ring. They dragged four large tumbling mats together, spreading them side by side to form a square close to the size of an actual ring. Astro went to one of the small lockers under the balcony and returned with two pairs of boxing gloves.

"Here," offered Astro, "put these on."

"Gloves?" asked Roger, in a voice of mock surprise. "I thought this was going to be a battle of blood."

"Any way you want it, Manning. Any way at all," said Tom.

"You're going to use gloves," growled Astro. "I don't want anybody killed." He threw a pair at each of them.

"There'll be three-minute rounds, with one minute rest," he continued. "Go off the mats and you'll be counted out. Usual rules otherwise. Any questions?"

"Clear to me, Astro," said Tom.

"Let's go," nodded Roger.

"One more thing," said Astro. "I hope Tom pins your ears back, Manning. But I'm going to see that both of you get a fair deal. So keep the punches up—and fight it out. All right—time!"

The two boys moved carefully to the center of the improvised ring, their guards up, while Astro stood off the edge of the mat and watched the sweeping second hand of his wrist chronograph.

Shuffling forward Tom pushed out a probing left and then tried to cross his right, but Manning stepped back easily, countering with a hard left to Tom's heart.

"I forgot to tell you, Corbett," he called out, "I'm considered a counterpuncher. I always—"

He was cut off with a sharp left to the face that snapped his head back, and his lips curled in a smile of condescension.

"Good—very good, Corbett."

Then with lightning speed and the grace of a cat, Roger slipped inside Tom's guard, punching hard and true. A left, a right and a left pounded into Tom's mid-section, and as he gave way momentarily Tom's face clouded over.

They circled. Tom kept leading with sharp lefts that popped in and out like a piston, always connecting and keeping Roger off balance. Roger concentrated on penetrating Tom's defense, methodically pounding his ribs and heart and trying to wear him down.

"Time!" bawled Astro.

The two boys dropped their hands and turned back to their corners. They squatted on the floor breathing slowly and easily. Astro stood in the middle of the ring, glaring at both of them in turn and shaking his head.

"Huh. I expected to see you two try to wallop each other into meteor dust! Keep fighting like that and we'll be here all night!"

"Talk to Corbett," sneered Roger. "Looks like he's afraid to mix it up!"

"You fight your way, Roger, and I'll fight mine," replied Tom, his voice cold and impersonal.

"Time!" suddenly yelled Astro and stepped back off the mat.

The two cadets jumped to their feet and met in the center of the ring again. With a bull-like rush, Roger changed tactics and began to rain punches all over Tom's body, but the curly-haired cadet stood his ground coolly, picking some off in mid-air with his gloves and sliding under the others. Then, as Roger slowed down, Tom took the offensive, popping his left into his opponent's face steadily and methodically, while keeping his right cocked for a clear opening to the chin.

Roger danced in and out, watching Tom's left as though it was a snake and trying unsuccessfully to get through his guard. But the sharp lefts kept snapping his head back and his face began to redden, not only from the sting of the blows but with the mounting fury of his frustration.

Suddenly, as Astro raised his arm to call time for the end of the round, Roger jumped forward and rained another series of harmless blows on Tom's shoulders and arms. But then, as the big Venusian called time, he stepped back and Tom dropped his guard. Instantly, Roger threw a right with all his weight behind it. It landed flush on Tom's jaw and he dropped, sprawling full length on the mats and lying still.

Smiling, Roger sauntered to his corner while Astro charged in and bent over the fallen cadet.

"None of that, Astro!" snapped Roger. "Since when does a referee take sides? Leave him alone! If he doesn't come out for the next round, you have to count him out!"

The big Venusian straightened and walked menacingly toward Roger's corner. "You hit him after I called time," he growled.

"So I have to take you on too, huh?" Roger jumped to his feet. "All right—come on, you big blast of space gas!"

"Wait, Astro . . . wait!"

Astro suddenly wheeled around to see Tom shaking his head weakly and trying to rise up on his elbows. He rushed back to the fallen boy's side.

Roger shouted at him angrily, "Leave him alone!"

"Ahhh—go blow your jets!" was Astro's snarling reply as he bent over Tom, who was now sitting up. "Tom, are you O.K.?"

"Yeah—yeah," he replied weakly. "But stay out of this. You're the referee. How much time left?"

"Twenty seconds," said Astro. "Roger smacked you after I called time."

"If he did, I didn't know a thing about it. I was out." Tom managed a cold smile. "Nice punch, Roger."

"Ten seconds," said Astro, stepping back off the mat.

"Thanks for the compliment, Corbett." Roger eyed the other cadet speculatively. "But are you sure you want to go on?"

"I was saved by the bell, wasn't I?"

"Yeah—sure—but if you'd rather quit—"

"Time!" cried Astro.

Tom rose to his feet—shook his head—and brought up his hands. He wasn't a moment too soon. Roger had rushed across the mat, trying to land another murderous right. Tom brought up his shoulder just in time, slipping with the punch, and at the same time, bringing up a terrific left to Roger's open mid-section. Manning let out a grunt and clinched. Tom pursued his advantage, pumping rights and lefts to the body, and he could feel the arrogant cadet weakening. Suddenly, Roger crowded in close, wrestling Tom around so that Astro was on the opposite side of the mat, then brought up his head under Tom's chin. The pop of Tom's teeth could be heard all over the great hall. Roger quickly stepped back, and back-pedaled until Astro called time.

"Thanks for teaching me that one, Roger. Learned two tricks from you today," said Tom, breathing heavily, but with the same cold smile on his face.

"That's all right, Corbett. Any time," said Manning.

"What tricks?" asked Astro. He looked suspiciously at Manning, who was doubled over, finding it hard to breath.

"Nothing I can't handle in time," said Tom, looking at Roger.

"Time!" called Astro and stepped off the mat.

The two boys got to their feet slowly. The pace was beginning to show on them and they boxed carefully.

The boys were perfectly matched, Tom constantly snapping Roger's head back with the jolting left jabs and following to the head or heart with a right cross. And Roger counterpunching, slipping hooks and body punches in under Tom's long leads. It was a savage fight. The three weeks of hard physical training had conditioned the boys perfectly.

At the end of the twelfth round, both boys showed many signs of wear. Roger's cheeks were as red as the glow of a jet blast deflector from the hundreds of lefts Tom had pumped into his face, while Tom's ribs and mid-section were bruised and raw where Roger's punches had landed successfully.

It couldn't last much longer, thought Astro, as he called time for the beginning of the thirteenth round.

Roger quickened his pace, dancing in and out, trying to move in under Tom's lefts, but suddenly Tom caught him with a right hand that was cocked and ready. It staggered him and he fell back, covering up. Tom pressed his advantage, showering rights and lefts everywhere he could find an opening. In desperation, his knees buckling, Roger clinched tightly, quickly brought up his open glove and gouged his thumb into Tom's eyes. Tom pulled back, instinctively pawing at his eye with his right glove. Roger, spotting the opening, took immediate advantage of it, shooting a hard looping right that landed flush on Tom's jaw. Tom went down.

Unaware of Roger's tactics, Astro jumped into the ring and his arm pumped the deadly count.

"One—two—three—four—"

It was going to be tough if Roger won, Astro thought, as he counted.

"Five—six—"

Arrogant enough now, he would be impossible to live with.

"Seven—eight—"

Tom struggled up to a sitting position and stared angrily at his opponent in the far corner.

"Nine—"

With one convulsive effort, Tom regained his feet. His left eye was closed and swollen, his right bleary with fatigue. He wobbled drunkenly on his feet. But he pressed forward. This was one fight he had to win.

Roger moved in for the finish. He slammed a left into Tom's shell, trying to find an opening for the last finishing blow. But Tom remained in his shell, forearms picking off the smashes that even hurt his arms, as he waited for the strength to return to his legs and arms and his head to clear. He knew that he couldn't go another round. He wouldn't be able to see. It would have to be this round, and he had to *beat* Roger. *Not* because he wanted to, but because Roger was a member of the unit. And he had to keep the unit together.

He circled his unit-mate with care, shielding himself from the shower of rights and lefts that rained around him. He waited—waited for the one perfect opening.

"Come on! Open up and fight, Corbett," panted Roger.

Tom snapped his right in reply. He noticed that Roger moved in with a hook every time he tried to cross his right. He waited—his legs began to shake. Roger circled and Tom shot out the left again, dropped into a semicrouch and feinted with the right cross. Roger moved in, cocking his fist for the left hook and Tom was ready for him. He threw the right, threw it with every ounce of strength left in his body. Roger was caught moving in and took the blow flush on the chin. He stopped as if poleaxed. His eyes turned glassy and then he dropped to the mat. He was out cold.

Astro didn't even bother to count.

Tom squatted on the mat beside Roger and rubbed the blond head with his glove.

"Get some water, Astro," he said, gasping for breath. "I'm glad I don't have to fight this guy again. And I'll tell you something else—"

"What?" asked Astro.

"Anybody that wants to win as much as this guy does, is going to win, and I want to have him on my side!"

Astro merely grunted as he turned toward the water cooler.

"Maybe," he called back. "But he ought to read a book of rules first!"

When he came back to the mat with the water, Roger was sitting up, biting the knots of the laces on his gloves. Tom helped him, and when the soggy leather was finally discarded, he stuck out his hand. "Well, Roger, I'm ready to forget everything we've said and start all over again."

Roger looked at the extended hand for a moment, his eyes blank and expressionless. Then, with a quick movement, he slapped it away and lurched to his feet.

"Go blow your jets," he snarled, and turning his back on them, stumbled across the gym.

Tom watched him go, bewilderment and pain mirrored on his face.

"I thought sure this would work, Astro," he sighed. "I thought he'd come to his senses if—"

"Nothing'll make that space creep come to his senses," Astro broke in disgustedly. "At least, nothing short of an atomic war head! Come on. Let's get you cleaned up!"

Putting his arm around Tom's shoulder, the big Venusian led him across the floor of the deserted gym, and as they disappeared through the automatic sliding doors, a tall figure in the uniform of the Solar Guard stepped out of the shadows on the balcony above. It was Captain Strong.

He stood silently at the rail, looking down at the mats and the soggy discarded boxing gloves. Tom had won the fight, he thought, but he had lost the war. The unit was now farther apart than it had ever been.

CHAPTER 6

"Well, Steve, how's everything going?"

Captain Steve Strong didn't answer right away. He returned the salute of a Space Cadet passing on the opposite slidewalk and then faced Commander Walters who stood beside him, eyeing him quizzically.

"Things are shaping up pretty well, Commander," he replied, finally, with an air of unconcern.

"The Earthworm units buckling down to business?" Commander Walters' voice matched Strong's in nonchalance.

"Yes, I'd say so, sir. Speaking generally, of course." Strong felt the back of his neck begin to flush as Walters kept eyeing him.

"And—speaking specifically, Steve?"

"Why—ah—what do you mean, sir?"

"Let's stop fencing with each other, Steve." Walters spoke kindly but firmly. "What about Manning and Unit 42-D? Are those boys learning to work together or not? And I want facts, not hopes!"

Strong hesitated, trying to word his reply. In these weeks that had followed Tom's fight with Roger in the gym, there had been no further incidents of open warfare. Roger's attitude, once openly defiant, had now subsided into a stream of never-ending sarcasm. The sting had been taken out of his attack and he seemed satisfied merely to annoy. Astro had withdrawn into a shell, refusing to allow Roger to bother him and only an occasional rumble of anger indicated his true feelings toward his troublesome unit-mate. Tom maintained his role of peacemaker and daily, in many ways, showed his capacity for leadership by steering his unit-mates away from any storm-provoking activities.

Strong finally broke the silence. "It's difficult to answer that question with facts, Commander Walters."

"Why?" insisted Walters.

"Well, nothing's really happened," answered Steve.

"You mean, nothing since the fight in the gym?"

"Oh—" Strong flushed. "You know about that?"

Commander Walters smiled. "Black eyes and faces that looked like raw beef don't go unnoticed, Steve."

"Uhh—no, sir," was Strong's lame reply.

"What I want to know is," pursued Walters, "did the fight prove anything? Did the boys get it out of their systems and are they concentrating on becoming a unit?"

"Right now, Commander, they're concentrating on passing their manuals. They realize that they have to work together to get through this series of tests. Why, Dr. Dale told me the other day that she's sure Tom's been giving Roger a few pointers on control-deck operation. And one night I found Manning giving Astro a lecture in compression ratios. Of course, Manning's way of talking is a way that would confuse the Venusian more than it would help him, but at least they weren't snarling at each other."

"Hmm," Walters nodded. "Sounds hopeful, but still not conclusive. After all, they have to help each other in the manuals. If one member of the unit fails, it will reflect on the marks of the other two and they might be washed out too. Even the deadliest enemies will unite to save their lives."

"Perhaps, sir," replied Strong. "But we're not dealing with deadly enemies now. These are three boys, with three distinct personalities who've been lumped together in strange surroundings. It takes time and patience to make a team that will last for years."

"You may have the patience, Steve, but the Academy hasn't the time." Commander Walters was suddenly curt. "When does Unit 42-D take its manuals?"

"This afternoon, sir," replied Strong. "I'm on my way over to the examination hall right now."

"Very well. I won't take any action yet. I'll wait for the results of the tests. Perhaps they will solve both our problems. See you later, Steve." Turning abruptly, Commander Walters stepped off the slidewalk onto the steps of the Administration Building and rapidly disappeared from view.

Left alone, Strong pondered the commander's parting statement. The implication was clear. If the unit failed to make a grade high enough to warrant the trouble it took keeping it together, it would be broken up. Or even worse, one or more of the boys would be dismissed from the Academy.

A few minutes later Strong arrived in the examination hall, a large, barren room with a small door in each of the three walls other than the one containing the entrance. Tom Corbett was waiting in the center of the hall and saluted smartly as Strong approached.

"Cadet Corbett reporting for manual examination, sir!"

"Stand easy, Corbett," replied Strong, returning the salute. "This is going to be a rough one. Are you fully prepared?"

"I believe so, sir." Tom's voice wasn't too steady.

A fleeting smile passed over Strong's lips, then he continued. "You'll take the control-deck examination first. Manning will be next on the radar bridge and Astro last on the power deck."

"They'll be here according to schedule, sir."

"Very well. Follow me."

Strong walked quickly to the small door in the left wall, Tom staying a respectful step behind. When they reached the door, the officer pressed a button in the wall beside it and the door slid open.

"All right, Corbett. Inside." Strong nodded toward the interior of the room.

The boy stepped in quickly, then stopped in amazement. All around him was a maze of instruments and controls. And in the center, twin pilot's chairs.

"Captain Strong!" Tom was so surprised that he could hardly get the words out. "It's—it's a real control deck!"

Strong smiled. "As real as we can make it, Corbett, without allowing the building to blast off." He gestured toward the pilot's chairs. "Take your place and strap in."

"Yes, sir." His eyes still wide with wonder, Tom stepped over to the indicated chair and Strong followed him, leaning casually against the other.

He watched the young cadet nervously adjust his seat strap and put a comforting hand on his shoulder. "Nervous, Corbett?"

"Yes, sir—just a little," replied Tom.

"Don't worry," said Strong. "You should have seen the way I came into this room fifteen years ago. My cadet officer had to help me into the control pilot's seat."

Tom managed a fleeting smile.

"Now, Corbett"—Strong's voice became businesslike—"as you know, these manual tests are the last tests before actually blasting off. In the past weeks, you cadets have been subjected to every possible examination, to discover any flaw in your work that might later crop up in space. This manual operations test of the control board, like Manning's on the radar bridge and Astro's on the power deck, is designed to test you under simulated space conditions. If you pass this test, your next step is real space."

"Yes, sir."

"I warn you, it isn't easy. And if you fail, you personally will wash out, and if other members of the unit do not get a high enough mark to average out to a passing grade for all of you, you fail as a unit."

"I understand, sir," said Tom.

"All right, then we'll begin. Your crew is aboard, the air lock is closed. What is the first thing you do?"

"Adjust the air circulating system to ensure standard Earth conditions."

"How do you do that?"

"By pressing this button which will activate the servo units. They automatically keep the circulating pumps in operation, based on thermostatic readings from the main gauge." Tom pointed to a black clock face, with a luminous white hand and numbers.

"All right, carry on," said Strong.

Tom reached over the huge control board that extended around him for some two feet on three sides. He placed a nervous finger on a small button, waited for the gauge below to register with a swing of the hand, and then released it. "All pressures steady, sir."

"What next?"

"Check the crew, sir—all departments—" replied Tom.

"Carry on," said Strong.

Tom reached out and pulled a microphone toward him.

"All hands! Station check!" said Tom, and then was startled to hear a metallic voice answer him.

"Power deck, ready for blast-off!" And then another voice: "Radar deck, ready for blast-off!"

Tom leaned back in the pilot's seat and turned to the captain. "All stations ready, sir."

"Good! What next?" asked Strong.

"Ask spaceport tower for blast-off clearance—"

Strong nodded. Tom turned back to the microphone, and without looking, punched a button in front of him.

"Rocket cruiser—" He paused and turned back to Strong. "What name do I give, sir?"

Strong smiled. "*Noah's Ark*—"

"Rocket cruiser *Noah's Ark* to spaceport control! Request blast-off clearance and orbit."

Once again a thin metallic voice answered him and gave the necessary instructions.

On and on, through every possible command, condition or decision that would be placed in front of him, Tom guided his imaginary ship on its imaginary flight through space. For two hours he pushed buttons, snapped switches and jockeyed controls. He gave orders and received them from the thin metallic voices. They answered him with such accuracy, and sometimes with seeming hesitation, that Tom found it difficult to believe that they were only electronically controlled recording devices. Once, when supposedly blasting through space at three-quarters space speed, he received a warning from the radar bridge of an approaching asteroid. He asked for a course change, but in reply received only static. Believing the recording to have broken down, he turned inquiringly to Captain Strong, but received only a blank stare in return. Tom hesitated for a split second, then turned back to the controls. He quickly flipped the teleceiver button on and began plotting the course of the approaching asteroid, ignoring for the moment his other duties on the control deck. When he had finished, he gave the course shift to the power deck and ordered a blast on the starboard jet. He waited for the course change, saw it register on the gauges in front of him, then continued his work.

Strong suddenly leaned over and clapped him on the back enthusiastically.

"Good work, Corbett. That broken recording was put there intentionally to trap you. Not one cadet in twenty would have had the presence of mind you showed in plotting the course of that asteroid yourself."

"Thank you, sir," stammered Tom.

"That's all—the test is over. Return to your quarters." He came over and laid a hand on Tom's shoulder. "And don't worry, Corbett. While it isn't customary to tell a cadet, I think you deserve it. You've passed with a perfect score!"

"I have, sir? You mean—*I really passed?*"

"Next step is Manning," said Strong. "You've done as much as one cadet can do."

"Thank you, sir"—Tom could only repeat it over and over—"thank you, sir—thank you."

Dazed, he saluted his superior and turned to the door. Two hours in the pilot's chair had made him dizzy. But he was happy.

Five minutes later he slammed back the sliding door and entered the quarters of 42-D with a lusty shout.

"Meet Space Cadet Corbett—an Earthworm who's just passed his control-deck manual operations exam!"

Astro looked up from a book of tables on astrogation and gave Tom a wan smile.

"Congratulations, Tom," he said, and turned back to his book, adding bitterly, "but if I don't get these tables down by this afternoon for my power-deck manual, you're sunk."

"Say—what's going on here?" asked Tom. "Where's Roger? Didn't he help you with them?"

"He left. Said he had to see someone before taking his radar-bridge manual. He helped me a little. But when I'd ask him a question, he'd just rattle the answer off so fast—well, I just couldn't follow him."

Suddenly slamming the book shut, he got up. "Me and these tables"—he indicated the book—"just don't mix!"

"What's the trouble?"

"Ah—I can get the easy ones about astrogation. They're simple. But it's the ones where I have to *combine* it with the power deck."

"Well—I mean—what specifically?" asked Tom softly.

"For instance, I've got to find the ratio for compression on the main firing tubes, using a given amount of fuel, heading for a given destination, and taking a given time for the passage."

"But that's control-deck operations—as well as astrogation and power!" exclaimed Tom.

"Yeah—I know," answered Astro, "but I've still got to be able to do it. If anything happened to you two guys and I didn't know how to get you home, then what?"

Tom hesitated. Astro was right. Each member of the unit had to depend on the other in any emergency. And if one of them failed . . . ? Tom saw why the ground manuals were so important now.

"Look," offered Tom. "Suppose we go over the whole thing again together. Maybe you're fouled up on the basic concept."

Tom grabbed a chair, hitched it close to the desk and pulled Astro down beside him. He opened the book and began studying the problem.

"Now look—you have twenty-two tons of fuel—and considering the position of your ship in space—"

As the two boys, their shoulders hunched over the table, began reviewing the table of ratios, across the quadrangle in the examination hall Roger Manning stood in a replica of a rocket ship's radar bridge and faced Captain Strong.

"Cadet Manning reporting for manual examination, sir." Roger brought up his arm in a crisp salute to Captain Strong, who returned it casually.

"Stand easy, Manning," replied Strong. "Do you recognize this room?"

"Yes, sir. It's a mock-up of a radar bridge."

"A workable mock-up, cadet!" Strong was vaguely irritated by Roger's nonchalance in accepting a situation that Tom had marveled at. "You will take your manuals here!"

"Yes, sir."

"On these tests you will be timed for both efficiency and speed and you'll use all the tables, charts and astrogation equipment that you'd find in a spaceship. Your problems are purely mathematical. There are no decisions to make. Just use your head."

Strong handed Roger several sheets of paper containing written problems. Roger shuffled them around in his fingers, giving each a quick glance.

"You may begin any time you are ready, Manning," said Strong.

"I'm ready now, sir," replied Roger calmly. He turned to the swivel chair located between the huge communications board, the adjustable chart table and the astrogation prism. Directly in front of him was the huge radar scanner, and to one side and overhead was a tube mounted on a swivel joint that looked like a small telescope, but which was actually an astrogation prism for taking sights on the celestial bodies in space.

Roger concentrated on the first problem.

". . . you are now in the northwest quadrant of Mars, chart M, area twenty-eight. You have been notified by the control deck that it has been necessary to jettison three quarters of your fuel supply. For the last five hundred and seventy-nine seconds you have been blasting at one-quarter space speed. The four main drive rockets were cut out at thirty-second intervals. Making adjustment for degree of slip on each successive rocket cutout, find present position by using cross-fix with Regulus as your starboard fix, Alpha Centauri as your port fix."

Suddenly a bell began to ring in front of Roger. Without hesitation he adjusted a dial that brought the radar scanner into focus. When the screen remained blank, he made a second adjustment, and then a third and fourth, until the bright white flash of a meteor was seen on the scanner. He quickly grabbed two knobs, one in each hand, and twisted them to move two thin, plotting lines, one horizontal and one vertical, across the surface of the scanner. Setting the vertical line, he fingered a tabulating machine with his right hand, as he adjusted the second line with his left, thus cross-fixing the meteor. Then he turned his whole attention to the tabulator, ripped off the answer with lightning moves of his fingers and began talking rapidly into the microphone.

"Radar bridge to control deck! Alien body bearing zero-one-five, one-point-seven degrees over plane of the ecliptic. On intersecting orbit. Change course two degrees, hold for fifteen seconds, then resume original heading. Will compensate for change nearer destination!"

Roger watched the scanner a moment longer. When the rumbling blast of the steering jets sounded in the chamber and the meteor flash shifted on the scanner screen, he returned to the problem in his hand.

Seven minutes later he turned to Strong and handed him the answer.

"Present position by dead reckoning is northwest quadrant of Mars, chart O, area thirty-nine, sir," he announced confidently.

"I was unable to get a sight on Alpha Centauri"

Strong tried to mask his surprise, but a lifted eyebrow gave him away. "And how did you arrive at this conclusion, Manning?"

"I was unable to get a sight on Alpha Centauri due to the present position of Jupiter, sir," replied Roger easily. "So I took a fix on Earth, allowed for its rotational speed around the sun and took the cross-fix with Regulus as ordered in the problem. Of course, I included all the other factors of the speed and heading of our ship. That was routine."

Strong accepted the answer with a curt nod, motioning for Roger to continue. It would not do, thought Strong, to let Manning know that he was the first cadet in thirty-nine years to make the correct selection of Earth in working up the fix with Regulus, and still have the presence of mind to plot a meteor without so much as a half-degree error. Of course the problem varied with each cadet, but it remained essentially the same.

"Seven-and-a-half minutes. Commander Walters will be surprised, to say the least," thought Steve.

Forty-five minutes later, Roger, as unruffled as if he had been sitting listening to a lecture from a sound slide, handed in the rest of his papers, executed a sharp salute and walked out.

"Two down and one to go," thought Strong, and the toughest one of them all coming up. Astro. The big Venusian was unable to understand anything that couldn't be turned with a wrench. The only thing that would prevent Unit 42-D from taking Academy unit honors over Unit 77-K, the unit assigned to Lieutenant Wolcheck, would be Astro. While none of the members of the other units could come up to the individual brilliance of Corbett or Manning, they worked together as a unit, helping one another. They might make a higher unit rating, simply because they were better balanced.

He shrugged his shoulders and collected the papers. It was as much torture for him, as it was for any cadet, he thought, and turned to the door. "All right, Astro," he said to himself, "in ten minutes it'll be your turn and I'm going to make it tough!"

Back in the quarters of Unit 42-D, Tom and Astro still pored over the books and papers on the desk.

"Let's try again, Astro," sighed Tom as he hitched his chair closer to the desk. "You've got thirty tons of fuel—you want to find the compression ratio of the number-one firing-tube chamber—so what do you do?"

"Start up the auxiliary, burn a little of the stuff and judge what it'll be," the big cadet replied. "That's the way I did it on the space freighters."

"But you're not on a space freighter now!" exclaimed Tom. "You've got to do things the way they want it done here at the Academy. By the book! These tables have been figured out by great minds to help you, and you just want to burn a little of the stuff and guess at what it'll be!" Tom threw up his hands in disgust.

"Seems to me I heard of an old saying back in the teen centuries about leading a horse to water, but not being able to make him drink!" drawled Roger from the doorway. He strolled in and kicked at the crumpled sheets of paper that littered the floor, stark evidence of Tom's efforts with Astro.

"All right, wise guy," said Tom, "suppose you explain it to him!"

"No can do," replied Roger. "I tried. I explained it to him twenty times this morning while you were taking your control-deck manual." He tapped his head delicately with his forefinger. "Can't get through—too thick!"

Astro turned to the window to hide the mist in his eyes.

"Lay off, Roger," snapped Tom. He got up and walked over to the big cadet. "Come on, Astro, we haven't got much time. You're due in the examination hall in a few minutes."

"It's no good, Tom, I just can't understand that stuff." Astro turned and faced his unit-mates, his voice charged with sudden emotion. "Just fifteen minutes on the power deck of anything with rockets in her and I'll run her from here to the next galaxy. I—I can't explain it, but when I look at those motors, I can read 'em like you read an astrogation chart, Roger, or you the gauges on the control deck, Tom. But I just can't get those ratios out of a book. I gotta put my hands on those motors—touch 'em—I mean really *touch 'em*—then I know what to do!"

As suddenly as he had started, he stopped and turned, leaving Tom and Roger staring at him, startled by this unusual outburst.

"Cadets—stand *to!*" roared a voice from the doorway.

The three cadets snapped to attention and faced the entrance.

"Take it easy, Earthworms!" said Tony Richards. A tall cadet with closely cut black hair and a lazy, smiling face stood in the doorway.

"Lay off, Richards," said Tom. "We haven't time for gags now. Astro's going to take his power-deck manual in a few minutes and we're cramming with him."

"O.K.—O.K.—don't blow your jets," said Richards. "I just wanted to see if there were any bets on which unit would cop honors in the manuals this afternoon."

"I suppose you think your Unit 77-K will finish on top?" drawled Roger.

"I'd like to bet all the galley demerits we have in 77-K against yours."

"With Astro on our team?" complained Roger.

"What's the matter with Astro?" asked Richards. "From what I hear, he's hot stuff!" It wasn't a compliment, but a sharp dig made with a sly smile. Astro balled his huge hands into fists.

"Astro," said Roger, "is the type that can smell out trouble on any power deck. But today he came down with a cold. No, I'm afraid it's no bet, Richards."

"I'll give you two to one," Richards offered.

"Nothing doing," replied Roger. "Not even at five to one. Not with Astro."

Richards grinned, nodded and disappeared.

Roger turned to face the hard stare of Tom.

"That was the dirtiest sellout I've ever heard, Manning," Tom growled.

"Sorry, Corbett," said Roger. "I only bet on sure things."

"That's O.K. with me, Manning," said Astro, "but I'm afraid you sold yourself a hot rocket, because I'm going to pass!"

"Who are you kidding?" Roger laughed and sprawled on his bunk.

Astro took a quick step forward, his fists clenched, his face a mask of burning anger, but Tom quickly jumped in front of him.

"You'll be late for the exam, Astro!" he shouted. "Get going or it'll count against your mark!"

"Huh. What's a few points more or less when you're going to fail anyway," snorted Roger from the bunk.

Again, Astro started to lunge forward and Tom braced himself against the Venusian's charge, but suddenly the burly cadet stopped. Disengaging Tom's restraining arms, he spoke coldly to the sneering boy on the bed.

"I'm going to pass the exam, Manning. Get that? I'm going to pass and then come back and beat your head off!" Turning on his heel, he stalked out of the room.

Tom immediately wheeled to face Roger, fire in his eyes, and the arrogant cadet, sensing trouble, jumped to his feet to meet him.

"What's the idea of giving Astro a hard time?" demanded Tom.

"Cool off, Corbett," replied Roger warily. "You're fusing your tubes you're so hot."

"You bet I'm hot! Hot enough to blast you—again!" Tom deliberately spat out the last word.

Roger flushed and brought his fists up quickly as though to charge in, then suddenly dropped them again. He turned to the door and slowly walked out.

"Go blow your jets," his voice drifted back to Tom as he disappeared.

Tom stood there, looking at the empty door, almost blind with rage and frustration. He was failing in the main job assigned to him, that of keeping the unit on an even keel and working together. How could he command a crew out in space if he couldn't keep the friction of his own unit under control?

Slowly, he left the room to wait for Astro in the recreation hall where the results of the manuals would be announced. He thought of Astro, now probably deep in his exam, and wondered how bad it would be for him. Then another thought crossed his mind. Roger had said nothing of his own test and neither he nor Astro had even inquired.

He shook his head. No matter where the unit placed in the manuals, it just couldn't stay together.

CHAPTER 7

It was customary for all Earthworm cadets to gather in the main recreation hall to wait for the results of the manuals which would be announced on the huge teleceiver screen. Since all the units were taking their tests that afternoon, the hall was crowded with green-clad cadets, talking in low murmurs and waiting tensely for the outcome of the exam.

Tom entered the huge room, looked around and then drifted toward Al Dixon, the senior cadet who had greeted them as a unit after passing classification tests. The blue-clad cadet was listening to a story spool, a device that told a story, rather than let the person read it from a book.

"Hiya, Corbett," said Dixon, smiling. "Drag up a chair. Listening to a terrific yarn about a guy stranded on an asteroid and then he finds—" The redheaded cadet's voice trailed off when he noticed that Tom wasn't listening.

"Say, what's the matter with you? You look like you just lost your best friend."

"Not yet, but it won't be long now," commented Tom, a trace of bitterness creeping into his voice. "Astro's taking his power-deck manual. What he knows about those compression ratios just isn't known. But he just can't get it on paper."

"Don't sell your unit-mate short," said Dixon, sensing something beneath Tom's comment. "I've heard that big fellow knows more about a rocket deck than McKenny."

"Yeah, that's true," said Tom, "but—"

"You know, Corbett," said Dixon, switching off the story spool, "there's something screwy in that outfit of yours."

"You can say that again," agreed Tom bitterly.

"You come in here with a face dragging on the floor, and Manning—"

Tom's head jerked up. "Manning! What about that space-gassing hot-shot?"

"—Manning just tore through the rec hall trying to get some of the other Earthworm units to bet their galley demerits against your outfit."

Tom's mouth sagged open. "You mean, he actually wanted to bet that Astro would pass?"

"Not just pass, Corbett, but he wanted to bet that your unit would be top rocket of the Earthworms! The head of the list!"

"But he told Astro that—" he stopped.

"Told him what?" Dixon asked.

"Ah—nothing—nothing—" said Tom. He jumped up and headed for the door.

"Hey, where are you going?"

"To find Manning. There are a couple of things I want to clear up."

Tom left Dixon shaking his head in bewilderment and jumped on the slidestairs. He was going to have it out with Roger once and for all. Hopping off the slidestairs onto the forty-second floor, he started down the long hall to his quarters.

Nearing the door, he heard Roger's laugh, and then his lazy voice talking to someone inside.

"Sure, they're dumb, but they're not bad guys," said Roger.

Tom walked into the room. Roger was sitting on the side of his bunk facing Tony Richards.

"Hiya, Corbett," said Roger, "did you hear how Astro made out yet?"

Tom ignored the question.

"I want to talk to you, Roger."

Roger eyed him suspiciously. "Sure, Corbett, go ahead."

"Well, I'll be going along," said Richards. He had heard about the previous fight between Manning and Corbett and didn't want to be hauled up as a witness later if they started again. "Remember, Manning," he called from the doorway, "the bet is two to one, and are you going to get tired of washing pots and pans!" He waved his hand at Corbett and disappeared.

"All right, Corbett," Roger turned to Tom. "What's frying you?"

"I just saw Al Dixon down in the rec hall," answered Tom. "He told me you were looking for bets on the unit ratings. Is that why Richards was here?"

"That's right," nodded Roger.

"What made you say the things you did to Astro before he went for his manual?"

"Very simple. I wanted to make him pass and that was the only way."

"You're pretty sure of yourself, Roger."

"I'm always sure of myself, Corbett. And the sooner you learn that, the easier it'll be for all of us. I never bet unless it's in the bag. I know Astro's going to pass. Some guys have to have a fire built under them before they get moving. Astro's one of them."

"That doesn't answer my question," said Tom. "Why did you say the things you did before a guy goes to take an exam?"

"I said what I did to make Tony Richards give me odds. *And* to make Astro mad enough to pass. We're a cinch to win and Richards' outfit will be indebted to us for a year's worth of galley demerits." He smiled easily. "Smooth, huh?"

"I think it's rotten," said Tom. "Astro left here feeling like a plugged credit! And if he does fail, it'll be because you made him think he was the dumbest guy in the universe!"

"He probably is," mused Roger, "but he still won't fail that manual."

From the hallway behind them, a loud blasting yell was suddenly heard, echoing from somewhere on the lower floors. Tom and Roger waited, their eyes wide and hopeful. There was only one person at Space Academy capable of making such a noise.

"He made it!" Tom exclaimed.

"Of course he made it," said Roger casually.

Astro tore into 42-D with a mad rush.

"Yeeeoooooowwww!" He grabbed the two cadets and picked them up, one in each hand. "I made it—hands down—I handled those rocket motors like they were babes in arms! I told you that all I had to do was touch them and I'd know! I told you!"

"Congratulations, Astro," said Tom with a wide grin. "I knew you'd do it."

"Put me down, you oversized Venusian jerk," said Roger, almost good-naturedly. Astro released the smaller cadet and faced him.

"Well, hot-shot, I promised you something when I got back, didn't I?"

"Make it later, will you, and I'll be glad to oblige." He walked toward the door. "I've got to go down and collect a bet."

"What bet?" asked Astro.

"With Tony Richards."

"But I thought you were afraid to bet on me!"

"Not at all, Astro. I just wanted to make you mad enough to ensure my winning."

"That sounds like you were more worried about your bet than you were about Astro passing," snapped Tom.

"You're exactly right, spaceboy," purred Roger, standing in the doorway.

"That's our boy, Manning," growled Astro. "The great team man!"

"Team?" Roger took a step back into the room. "Don't make me laugh, Astro. For your information, tomorrow morning I'm putting in for a transfer to another unit!"

"What!" exclaimed Tom. "You can't trans—"

"Yes, I can," interrupted Roger. "Read your Academy regs. Anyone can request a transfer once the unit has passed its manuals."

"And what excuse are you going to use," snapped Astro bitterly. "That you can't take it?"

"A personality difference, Astro, my boy. You hate me and I hate you. It's a good enough reason, I think."

"It's just as well, hot-shot," replied Astro. "Because if you don't transfer, we will!"

Roger merely smiled, flipped his fingers to his forehead in an arrogant gesture of farewell and turned to leave again. But his path was blocked by the sudden appearance of Captain Steve Strong. The three cadets quickly braced.

The Solar Guard officer strode into the room, his face beaming. He looked at each of the boys, pride shining out of his eyes, and then brought his hand up and held it in salute.

"I just want to tell you boys one thing," he said solemnly. "It's the highest compliment I can pay you, or anyone." He paused. "All three of you are real spacemen!"

Tom and Astro couldn't repress smiles, but Roger's expression never changed.

"Then we passed as a unit, sir?" asked Tom eagerly.

"Not only passed, Corbett"—Strong's voice boomed in the small room—"but with honors. You're the top rockets of this Earthworm group! I'm proud to be your commanding officer!"

Again Tom and Astro fought back smiles of happiness and even Roger managed a small grin.

"This is the fightingest group of cadets I've ever seen," Strong continued. "Frankly, I was a little worried about your ability to pull together but the results of the manuals showed that you have. You couldn't have made it without working as a unit."

Strong failed to notice Roger's face darken, and Tom and Astro look at each other meaningfully.

"My congratulations for having solved that problem too!" Strong saluted them again and walked toward the door, where he paused. "By the way, I want you to report to the Academy spaceport tomorrow at eight hundred hours. Warrant Officer McKenny has something out there he wants to show you."

Tom's eyes bugged out and he stepped forward.

"Sir," he gasped, scarcely able to get the question past his lips, "you don't mean we're—we're going to—"

"You're absolutely right, Corbett. There's a brand-new rocket cruiser out there. Your ship. Your future classroom. You'll report to her in the blues of the Space Cadets! And from now on your unit identification is the name of your ship! The rocket cruiser *Polaris*!"

A second later, Strong had vanished down the corridor, leaving Tom and Astro hugging each other and clapping each other on the back in delirious joy.

Roger merely stood to one side, a sarcastic smile on his face.

"And now, as we prepare to face the unknown dangers of space," he said bitingly, "let us unite our voices and sing the Academy hymn together! Huh!" He strode toward the door. "Don't they ever get tired of waving that flag around here?"

Before Tom and Astro could reply, he had disappeared. The big Venusian shrugged his shoulders. "I just don't understand that guy!"

But Tom failed to reply. He had turned toward the window and was staring out past the gleaming white Tower of Galileo into the slowly darkening skies of evening to the east. For the moment, the problems of Roger Manning and the unit were far away. He was thinking of the coming morning when he would dress in the blues of a Space Cadet for the first time and step into his own ship as command pilot. He was thinking of the morning when he would be a real spaceman!

CHAPTER 8

The campus of Space Academy was quiet that evening. Only a few cadets were still out on the quadrangle, lounging around in the open before returning to their quarters for bed-check.

On the forty-second floor of the dormitory building, two thirds of the newly formed *Polaris* unit, Tom and Astro, were in heated argument.

"All right, all right, so the guy is brilliant," said Astro. "But who can live with him? Not even himself!"

"Maybe he is a little difficult," replied Tom, "but somehow, we've got to adjust to him!"

"How about him adjusting to us? It's two against one!" Astro shambled to the window and looked out moodily. "Besides, he's putting in for a transfer and there's nothing we can do about it!"

"Maybe he won't now—not after that little speech Captain Strong made this afternoon."

"If he doesn't, then, blast it, I will!"

"Aw, now take it easy, Astro!"

"Take it easy, nothing!" Astro was building up a big head of steam. "Where is that space crawler right now?"

"I don't know. He never came back. Wasn't even down at mess tonight."

"There, that's just what I mean!" Astro turned to Tom to press his point. "It's close to bed-check and he isn't in quarters yet. If the MP's catch him outside after hours, the whole unit will be logged and there goes our chance of blasting off tomorrow!"

"But there's still time, Astro," replied Tom lamely.

"Not much there isn't. It just shows you what he thinks of the unit! He just doesn't care!" Astro paced the floor angrily. "There's only one thing to do! He gets his transfer—or we do! Or—" he paused and looked at Tom meaningfully, "or I do."

"You're not thinking, Astro," argued Tom. "How will that look on your record? Every time there's a trip into deep space, they yank out your file to see how you operate under pressure with other guys. When they see that you asked for a transfer from your unit, that's it!"

"Yeah—yeah—I know—incompatible—but honest, Tom—"

The curly-haired cadet felt his big friend weaken and he pressed his advantage.

"It isn't every day that a unit gets a ship right after finishing ground manuals. Captain Strong said he waited for four months after manuals before getting his first hop into space."

"Yeah—but what do you think it's going to be like out in space with Manning making sour cracks all the time?"

Tom hesitated before answering his Venusian friend. He was fully aware that Roger was going to play a lone hand. And that they would never really have unity among them until some drastic measure was taken. After all, Tom thought, some guys don't have good hearts, or eyes, a defect to prevent them from becoming spacemen. Roger is just mixed up inside. And the handicap is just as real as if he had a physical flaw.

"Well, what do you want to do?" asked Tom finally.

"Go see Captain Strong. Give it to him straight. Tell him we want a transfer."

"But tomorrow we blast off. We might not have another chance for months! Certainly not until we get a new astrogator."

"I'd rather wait and have a guy on the radar bridge I know isn't going to pull something behind my back," said Astro, "than blast off tomorrow with Manning aboard."

Again Tom hesitated. He knew what Astro was saying was the truth. Life, so far, at the Academy had been tough enough, but with mutual dependence and security even more important out in space, the danger of their constant friction was obvious.

"O.K.," he relented, "if that's the way you really want it. Come on. We'll go see Captain Strong now."

"You go," said Astro. "You know how I feel. Whatever you say goes for me too."

"Are you sure you want to do it?" asked Tom. He knew what such a request would mean. A black mark against Roger for being rejected by his unit-mates and a black mark against Astro and himself for not being able to adjust. Regardless of who was right and who was wrong, there would always be a mark on their records.

"Look, Tom," said Astro, "if I thought it was only me I'd keep my mouth shut. But you'd let Manning get away with murder because you wouldn't want to be the one to get him into trouble."

"No, I wouldn't," said Tom. "I think Roger would make a fine spaceman; he's certainly smart enough, and a good unit-mate if he'd only snap out of it. But I can't let him or anyone else stop me from becoming a spaceman or a member of the Solar Guard."

"Then you'll go see Captain Strong?"

"Yes," said Tom. If he had been in doubt before, now that he had made the decision, he felt relieved. He slipped on his space boots and stood up. The two boys looked at each other, each realizing the question in the other's mind.

"No!" said Tom decisively. "It's better for everyone. Even Roger. He might find two other guys that will fit him better." He walked from the room.

The halls were silent as he strode toward the slidestairs that would take him to the nineteenth floor and Captain Strong's quarters. Passing one room after another, he glanced in and saw other units studying, preparing for bed, or just sitting around talking. There weren't many units left. The tests had taken a toll of the Earthworms. But those that remained were solidly built. Already friendships had taken deep root. Tom found himself wishing he had become a member of another unit. Where the comradeship was taken for granted in other units, he was about to make a request to dissolve his because of friction.

Completely discouraged, Tom stepped on the slidestairs and started down.

As he left the dormitory floors, the noise of young cadet life was soon lost and he passed floors containing offices and apartments of the administration staff of the Solar Guard.

As he drew level with the floor that was Galaxy Hall, he glanced at the lighted plaque and for the hundredth time reread the inscription—

" . . . to the brave men who sacrificed their lives in the conquest of space, this Galaxy Hall is dedicated . . ."

Something moved in the darkness of the hall. Tom strained his eyes for a closer look and just managed to distinguish the figure of a cadet standing before the wreckage of the *Space Queen*. Funny, thought Tom. Why should anyone be wandering around the hall at this time of night? And then, as the floor slipped past, the figure turned slightly and was illuminated by the dim light that came from the slidestairs. Tom recognized the sharp features and close-cropped blond hair of Roger Manning!

Roger was still standing in front of the Space Queen!

Quickly changing over to the slidestairs going up, Tom slipped back to the hall floor and stepped off. Roger was still standing in front of the *Space Queen*!

Tom started to speak, but stopped when he saw Roger take out a handkerchief and dab at his eyes.

The movements of the other boy were crystal-clear to Tom. Roger was crying! Standing in front of the *Space Queen* and crying!

He kept watching as Roger put away the handkerchief, saluted sharply and turned toward the slidestairs. Ducking behind a glass case that held the first space suit ever used, Tom held his breath as Roger passed him. He could hear Roger mumble.

"They got you—but they won't get me with any of that glory stuff!"

Tom waited, heart racing, trying to figure out what Roger meant, and why he was here alone in Galaxy Hall. Finally the blond cadet disappeared up the moving stair.

Tom didn't go to see Captain Strong. Instead, he returned to his room.

"So quick?" asked Astro.

Tom shook his head. "Where's Roger?" he asked.

"In the shower." Astro gestured to the bathroom, where Tom could hear the sound of running water. "What made you change your mind about seeing Captain Strong?" asked Astro.

"I think we've misjudged Roger, Astro," said Tom slowly. And then related what he had seen and heard.

"Well, blast my jets!" exclaimed Astro, when Tom had finished. "What's behind it, do you think?"

"I don't know, Astro. But I'm convinced that any guy that'll visit Galaxy Hall by himself late at night—and *cry*—well, he couldn't be entirely off base, regardless of what he does."

Astro studied his work-hardened palms.

"You wanta keep it this way for a while?" he asked. "I mean, forget about talking to Captain Strong?"

"Roger's the best astrogator and radar man in the Academy, Astro. There's something bothering him. But I'm willing to bet that whatever it is, Roger will work it out. And if we're really unit-mates, then we won't sell him out now, when he may need us most."

"That's it, then," said Astro. "I'll kill him with kindness. Come on. Let's turn in. We've got a big day ahead of us tomorrow!"

The two boys began to prepare for bed. Roger came out of the shower wearing pajamas.

"All excited, spacemen?" he drawled, leaning against the wall, brushing his short hair.

"About as excited as we can get, Roger," smiled Tom.

"Yeah, you space-blasting jerk!" growled Astro good-naturedly. "Turn out the lights before I introduce you to my space boot."

Roger eyed the two cadets quizzically, puzzled by the strange good humor of both boys. He shrugged his shoulders, flipped out the light and crawled into bed.

But if he could have seen the satisfied smile of Tom Corbett, Roger would have been even more puzzled.

"We'll just kill him with kindness," thought Tom, and fell fast asleep.

CHAPTER 9

The three members of the *Polaris* unit stepped off the slidewalk at the Academy spaceport and stood before Warrant Officer McKenny.

"There she is," said the stubby spaceman, pointing to the gleaming spaceship resting not two hundred feet away. "Rocket cruiser *Polaris*. The newest and fastest ship in space."

He faced the three boys with a smile. "And she's all yours. You earned her!"

Mouths open, Tom, Roger and Astro stood gaping in fascination at the mighty spaceship resting on the concrete ramp. Her long two-hundred-foot polished beryllium steel hull mirrored the spaceport scene around them. The tall buildings of the Academy, the "ready" line of space destroyers and scouts, and the hundreds of maintenance noncoms of the enlisted Solar Guard, their scarlet uniforms spotted with grime, were all reflected back to the *Polaris* unit as they eyed the sleek ship from the needlelike nose of her bow to the stubby opening of her rocket exhausts. Not a seam or rivet could be seen in her hull. At the top of the ship, near her nose, a large blister made of six-inch clear crystal indicated the radar bridge. Twelve feet below it, six round window ports showed the position of the control deck. Surrounding the base of the ship was an aluminum scaffold with a ladder over a hundred feet high anchored to it. The top rung of the ladder just reached the power-deck emergency hatch which was swung open, like a giant plug, revealing the thickness of the hull, nearly a foot.

"Well," roared the red-clad spaceman, "don't you want to climb aboard and see what your ship looks like inside?"

"Do we!" cried Tom, and made a headlong dash for the scaffold. Astro let out one of his famous yells and followed right at his heels. Roger watched them running ahead and started off at a slow walk, but suddenly, no longer able to resist, he broke into a dead run. Those around the *Polaris* stopped their work to watch the three cadets scramble up the ladder. Most of the ground crew were ex-spacemen like McKenny, no longer able to blast off because of acceleration reaction. And they smiled knowingly, remembering their reactions to their first spaceship.

Inside the massive cruiser, the boys roamed over every deck, examining the ship excitedly.

"Say look at this!" cried Tom. He stood in front of the control board and ran his hands over the buttons and switches. "This board makes the manual we worked on at the Academy look like it's ready for Galaxy Hall!"

"Yeeeoooooww!" Three decks below, Astro had discovered the rocket motors. Four of the most powerful ever installed on a spaceship, enabling the *Polaris* to outrace any ship in space.

Roger stuck his head through the radar-bridge hatch and gazed in awe at the array of electronic communicators, detection radar and astrogation gear. With lips pulled into a thin line, he mumbled to himself: "Too bad they didn't give *you* this kind of equipment."

"What'd you say, Roger?" asked Astro, climbing alongside to peer into the radar bridge.

Startled, Roger turned and stammered, "Ah—nothing—nothing."

Looking around, Astro commented, "This place looks almost as good as that power deck."

"Of course," said Roger, "they could have placed that astrogation prism a little closer to the chart table. Now I'll have to get up every time I want to take sights on stars!"

"Don't you ever get tired of complaining?" asked Astro.

"Ah—rocket off," snarled Roger.

"Hey, you guys," yelled Tom from below, "better get down here! Captain Strong's coming aboard."

Climbing back down the ladder to the control deck, Astro leaned over his shoulder and asked Roger, "Do you really think he'll let us take this baby up for a hop, Manning?"

"Get your head out of that cloud, Astro. You'll pull about three weeks of dry runs before this baby gets five inches off the ground."

"I wouldn't be too sure of that, Manning!" Strong's voice boomed out as he climbed up through the control-deck hatch. The three boys immediately snapped to attention.

Strong walked around the control deck, fingering the controls lightly.

"This is a fine ship," he mused aloud. "One of the finest that scientific brains can build. She's yours. The day you graduate from the Academy, IF you graduate, and I can think of about a thousand reasons why you won't, you'll command an armed rocket cruiser similar to this. As a matter of fact, the only difference between this ship and those that patrol the space lanes now is in the armament."

"Don't we have any arms aboard at all, sir?" asked Tom.

"Small arms, like paralo-ray pistols and paralo-ray rifles. Plus four atomic war heads for emergency use," replied Strong.

Seeing a puzzled expression cross Astro's face, the Solar Guard officer continued, "You haven't studied armament yet, Astro, but paralo rays are the only weapons used by law-enforcement agencies in the Solar Alliance. They work on a principle of controlled energy, sending out a ray with an effective range of fifty yards that can paralyze the nervous system of any beast or human."

"And it doesn't kill, sir?" inquired Astro.

"No, Astro." replied Strong. "Paralyzing a man is just as effective as killing him. The Solar Alliance doesn't believe you have to kill anyone, not even the most vicious criminal. Freeze him and capture him, and you still have the opportunity of making him a useful citizen."

"But if you can't?" inquired Roger dryly.

"Then he's kept on the prison asteroid where he can't harm anyone." Strong turned away abruptly. "But this isn't the time for a general discussion. We've got work to do!"

He walked over to the master control panel and switched the teleceiver screen. There was a slight buzz, and a view of the spaceport outside the ship suddenly came into focus, filling the screen. Strong flipped a switch and a view aft on the *Polaris* filled the glowing square. The aluminum scaffolding was being hauled away by a jet truck. Again the view changed as Strong twisted the dials in front of him.

"Just scanning the outside, boys," he commented. "Have to make sure there isn't anyone near the ship when we blast off. The rocket exhaust is powerful enough to blow a man two hundred feet, to say nothing of burning him to death."

"You mean, sir—" began Tom, not daring to hope.

"Of course, Corbett," smiled Strong. "Take your stations for blast-off. We raise ship as soon as we get orbital clearance from spaceport control!"

Without waiting for further orders, the three boys scurried to their stations.

Soon the muffled whine of the energizing pumps on the power deck began to ring through the ship, along with the steady beep of the radar scanner on the radar bridge. Tom checked the maze of gauges and dials on the control board. Air locks, hatches, oxygen supply, circulating system, circuits, and feeds. In five minutes the two-hundred-foot shining steel hull was a living thing as her rocket motors purred, warming up for the initial thrust.

Tom made a last sweeping check of the complicated board and turned to Captain Strong who stood to one side watching.

"Ship ready to blast off, sir," he announced. "Shall I check stations and proceed to raise ship?"

"Carry on, Cadet Corbett," Strong replied. "Log yourself in as skipper with me along as supercargo. I'll ride in the second pilot's chair."

Tom snapped a sharp salute and added vocally, "Aye, aye, sir!"

He turned back to the control board, strapped himself into the command pilot's seat and opened the circuit to the spaceport control tower.

"Rocket cruiser *Polaris* to spaceport control," he droned into the microphone. "Check in!"

"Spaceport control to *Polaris*," the voice of the tower operator replied. "You are cleared for blast-off in two minutes. Take out— orbit 75 . . . repeat . . . 75 . . ."

"*Polaris* to spaceport control. Orders received and understood. End transmission!"

Tom then turned his attention to the station check.

"Control deck to radar deck. Check in."

"Radar deck, aye! Ready to raise ship." Roger's voice was relaxed, easy.

Tom turned to the board to adjust the teleceiver screen for a clear picture of the stern of the ship. Gradually it came up in as sharp detail as if he had been standing on the ground.

He checked the electric timing device in front of him that ticked off the seconds, as a red hand crawled around to *zero*, and when it swept down to the thirty-second mark, Tom pulled the microphone to his lips again. "Control deck to power deck. Check in!"

"Power deck, aye?"

"Energize the cooling pumps!"

"Cooling pumps, aye!" repeated Astro.

"Feed reactant!"

"Reactant at D-9 rate."

From seventy feet below them, Strong and Tom heard the hiss of the reactant mass feeding into the rocket motors, and the screeching whine of the mighty pumps that kept the mass from building too rapidly and exploding.

The second hand swept up to the twenty-second mark.

"Control deck to radar deck," called Tom. "Do we have a clear trajectory forward?"

"All clear forward and overhead," replied Roger.

Tom placed his hand on the master switch that would throw the combined circuits, instruments and gauges into the single act of blasting the mighty ship into space. His eyes glued to the sweeping hand, he counted past the twelve-second mark—eleven—ten—nine—

"Stand by to raise ship," he bawled into the microphone. "Minus—five—four—three—two—one—*zero!*"

Tom threw the master switch.

There was a split-second pause and then the great ship roared into life. Slowly at first, she lifted her tail full of roaring jets free of the ground. Ten feet—twenty—fifty—a hundred—five hundred—a thousand—picking up speed at an incredible rate.

Tom felt himself being pushed deeper and deeper into the softness of the acceleration cushions. He had been worried about not being able to keep his eyes open to see the dwindling Earth in the teleceiver over his head, but the tremendous force of the rockets pushing him against gravity to tear the two hundred tons of steel away from the Earth's grip held his eyelids open for him. As the powerful rockets tore deeper into the gap that separated the ship from Earth, he saw the spaceport gradually grow smaller. The rolling hills around the Academy closed in, and then the Academy itself, with the Tower of Galileo shrinking to a white stick, was lost in the brown and green that was Earth. The rockets pushed harder and harder and he saw the needle of the acceleration gauge creep slowly up. Four—five—six—seven—eight—nine—ten miles a second!

When the awful crushing weight on his body seemed unbearable, when he felt as though he would never be able to draw another breath, suddenly the pressure lifted and Tom felt amazingly and wonderfully buoyant. He seemed to be floating in mid-air, his body rising against the webbed straps of his chair! With a start and a momentary wave of panic, he realized that he *was* floating! Only the straps kept him from rising to the ceiling of the control room!

Recovering quickly, he realized that he was in free fall. The ship had cleared the pull of earth's gravity and was out in space where everything was weightless. Reaching toward the control panel, he flipped the switch for the synthetic-gravity generator and, seconds later, felt the familiar and reassuring sensation of the chair under him as the generator supplied an artificial-gravity field to the ship.

As he loosened the straps in his chair, he noticed Captain Strong rising from his position beside him and he grinned sheepishly in answer to the twinkle in Strong's eye.

"It's all right, Tom," reassured Strong. "Happens to everyone the first time. Carry on."

"Aye, aye, sir," replied Tom and he turned to the microphone. "Control deck to all stations! We are in space! Observe standard cruise procedure!"

"Power deck, aye!" was Astro's blasting answer over the loudspeaker. "Yeeeoooww! Out where we belong at last."

"Radar bridge here," Roger's voice chimed in softly on the speaker. "Everything under control. And, Astro, you belong in a zoo if you're going to bellow like that!"

"Ahhh—rocket off, bubblehead!" The big Venusian's reply was good-natured. He was too happy to let Roger get under his skin.

"All right, you two," interrupted Tom. "Knock it off. We're on a ship now. Let's cut the kindergarten stuff!"

"Aye, aye, skipper!" Astro was irrepressible.

"Yes, *sir*!" Roger's voice was soft but Tom recognized the biting edge to the last word.

Turning away from the controls, he faced Captain Strong who had been watching quietly.

"*Polaris* space-borne at nine hundred thirty-three hours, Captain Strong. All stations operating efficiently."

"Very competent job, Corbett," nodded Strong in approval. "You handled the ship as if you'd been doing it for years."

"Thank you, sir."

"We'll just cruise for a while on this orbit so you boys can get the feel of the ship and of space." The Solar Guard officer took Tom's place in the command pilot's chair. "You knock off for a while. Go up to the radar bridge and have a look around. I'll take over here."

"Yes, sir." Tom turned and had to restrain himself from racing up the ladder to the radar bridge. When he climbed through the hatch to Roger's station, he found his unit-mate tilted back in his chair, staring through the crystal blister over his head.

"Hiya, spaceboy," smiled Roger. He indicated the blister. "Take a look at the wide, deep and high."

Tom looked up and saw the deep blackness that was space.

"It's like looking into a mirror, Roger," he breathed in awe. "Only there isn't any other side—no reflection. It just doesn't stop, does it?"

"Nope," commented Roger, "it just goes on and on and on. And no one knows where it stops. And no one can even guess."

"Ah—you've got a touch of space fever," laughed Astro. "You'd better take it easy, pal."

Tom suppressed a smile. Now, for the first time, he felt that there was a chance to achieve unity among them. Kill him with kindness, he thought, that's the way to do it.

"All right, boys!" Captain Strong's voice crackled over the speaker. "Time to pull in your eyeballs and get to work again. We're heading back to the spaceport! Take your stations for landing!"

Tom and Astro immediately jumped toward the open hatch and started scrambling down the ladder toward their respective stations while Roger strapped himself into his chair in front of the astrogation panel.

Within sixty seconds the ship was ready for landing procedure and at a nod from Captain Strong, who again strapped himself into the second pilot's chair, Tom began the delicate operation.

Entering Earth's atmosphere, Tom gave a series of rapid orders for course changes and power adjustments, and then, depressing the master turn control, spun the ship around so that she would settle stern first toward her ramp at the Academy spaceport.

"Radar deck to control deck," called Roger over the intercom. "One thousand feet to touchdown!"

"Control deck, aye," answered Tom. "Control deck to power deck. Check in."

"Power deck, aye," replied Astro.

"Stand by to adjust thrust to maximum drive at my command," ordered Tom.

"Power deck, aye."

The great ship, balanced perfectly on the hot exhaust, slowly slipped toward the ground.

"Five hundred feet to touchdown," warned Roger.

"Main rockets full blast," ordered Tom.

The sudden blast of the powerful jets slowed the descent of the ship, and finally, fifty feet above the ground, Tom snapped out another order.

"Cut main rockets! Hold auxiliary!"

A moment later there was a gentle bump and the *Polaris* rested on the ramp, her nose pointed to the heavens.

"*Touchdown!*" yelled Tom. "Cut everything, fellas, and come up and sign the log. We made it—our first hop into space! We're spacemen!"

CHAPTER 10

"The next event will be," Warrant Officer McKenny's voice boomed over the loud-speaker and echoed over the Academy stadium, "the last semifinal round of mercuryball. *Polaris* unit versus *Arcturus* unit."

As two thousand space cadets, crowded in the grandstands watching the annual academy tournament, rose to their feet and cheered lustily, Tom Corbett turned to his unit-mates Astro and Roger and called enthusiastically, "O.K., fellas. Let's go out there and show them how to play this game!"

During the two days of the tournament, Tom, Roger and Astro, competing as a unit against all the other academy units, had piled up a tremendous amount of points in all the events. But so had Unit 77-K, now known as the *Capella* unit. Now with the *Capella* unit already in the finals, the *Polaris* crew had to win their semifinal round against the *Arcturus*, in order to meet the *Capella* in the final round for Academy honors.

"This is going to be a cinch," boasted Astro. "I'm going to burn 'em up!"

"Save it for the field," said Tom with a smile.

"Yeah, you big Venusian ape," added Roger. "Make points instead of space gas."

Stripped to the waist, wearing shorts and soft, three-quarter-length space boots, the three boys walked onto the sun-baked field amid the rousing cheers from the stands. Across the field, the cadets of the *Arcturus* unit walked out to meet them, stopping beside McKenny at the mid-field line. Mike waited for the six boys to form a circle around him, while he held the mercuryball, a twelve-inch plastic sphere, filled with air and the tricky tube of mercury.

"You all know the rules," announced McKenny abruptly. "Head, shoulders, feet, knees, or any part of your body except your hands, can touch the ball. *Polaris* unit will defend the north goal," he said, pointing to a white chalk line fifty yards away, "*Arcturus* the south," and he pointed to a line equally distant in the opposite direction. "Five-minute periods, with one-minute rest between. All clear?"

As captain of the *Polaris* unit, Tom nodded, while smiling at the captain of the *Arcturus* team, a tow-headed boy with short chunky legs named Schohari.

"All clear, Mike," said Tom.

"All clear here, Mike," responded Schohari.

"All right, shake hands and take your places."

The six boys shook hands and jogged toward respective opposite lines. Mike waited for them to reach their goal lines, and then placed the ball in the middle of a chalk-drawn circle.

Toeing the line, Tom, Roger and Astro eyed the *Arcturus* crew and prepared for the dash to the ball.

"All right, fellas," urged Tom, "let's show them something!"

"Yeah," breathed Astro, "just let me get my size thirteens on that pumpkin before it starts twisting around!"

Astro wanted the advantage of the first kick at the ball while the mercury tube inside was still quiet. Once the mercury was agitated, the ball would be as easy to kick as a well-greased eel.

"We'll block for you, Astro," said Tom, "and you put every ounce of beef you've got into that first kick. If we're lucky, we might be able to get the jump on them!"

"Cut the chatter," snapped Roger nervously. "Baldy's ready to give us the go ahead!"

Standing on the side lines, Warrant Officer McKenny slowly raised his hand, and the crowd in the grandstand hushed in eager anticipation. A second passed and then there was a tremendous roar as he brought his hand down and blew heavily on the whistle.

Running as if their lives depended on it, the six cadets of the two units raced headlong toward the ball. Tom, just a little faster than Roger or Astro, flashed down the field and veered off to block the advancing Schohari. Roger, following him, charged into Swift, the second member of the *Arcturus* crew. Astro, a few feet in back of them, running with surprising speed for his size, saw that it was going to be a close race between himself and Allen, the third member of the *Arcturus* unit. He bowed his head and drove himself harder, the roar of the crowd filling his ears.

"... Go Astro! ... Go Astro! ..."

Pounding down for the kick, Astro gauged his stride perfectly and with one last, mighty leap swung his right foot at the ball.

There was a loud thud drowned by a roar from the crowd as the ball sailed off the ground with terrific force. And then almost immediately there was another thud as Allen rose in a desperate leap to block the ball with his shoulder. It caromed off at a crazy angle, wobbling in its flight as the mercury within rolled from side to side. Swift, of the *Arcturus* crew, reached the ball first and sent it sailing at an angle over Tom's head to bounce thirty feet away. Seeing Astro charge the ball, Tom threw a block on Allen to knock him out of the play. The big Venusian, judging his stride to be a little off, shortened his steps to move in for the kick. But just as he brought his foot forward to make contact, the ball spun away to the left. Astro's foot continued in a perfect arc over his head, throwing him in a heap on the ground.

Two thousand voices from the stands roared in one peal of laughter.

While Astro lay on the ground with the wind knocked out of him, Schohari and Swift converged on the ball. With Astro down and Tom out of position, the *Arcturus* unit seemed certain of scoring. But again the ball rolled crazily, this time straight to Roger, the last defender. He nudged it between his opponents toward Tom, who, in turn, kicked it obliquely past Allen back to Roger again. Running with the grace and speed of an antelope, the blond cadet met the ball in mid-field, and when it dropped to the ground in front of him, sent it soaring across the goal with one powerful kick!

As the cadets in the stands sent up a tumultuous cheer for the perfectly executed play, the whistle blew, ending the period and the *Polaris* unit led, one to nothing.

Breathing deeply, Astro and Roger flopped down near Tom and stretched full length on the grass.

"That was a beautiful shot, Roger," said Tom. "Perfectly timed!"

"Yeah, hot-shot," agreed Astro, "I'm glad to see that big head of yours is good for something!"

"Listen, fellas," said Roger eagerly, ignoring Astro, "to go into the finals against Richards and the *Capella* unit, we've got to beat the *Arcturus* crew, right?"

"Yeah," agreed Tom, "and it won't be easy. We just happened to get the breaks."

"Then why don't we put the game on ice?" said Roger. "Freeze the ball! We got 'em one to nothing, that's enough to beat them. When the whistle blows and it's over, we win!"

Astro looked at Tom, who frowned and replied, "But we've still got three periods left, Roger. It isn't fair to freeze this early in the game. If it was the last minute or so, sure. But not so early. It just isn't fair."

"What do you want to do?" snarled Roger. "Win, or play fair?"

"Win, of course, but I want to win the right way," said Tom.

"How about you, Astro?" asked Roger.

"I feel the same way that Tom does," said the big cadet. "We can beat these guys easily—and on the square."

"You guys make it sound like I was cheating," snapped Roger.

"Well," said Tom, "it sure isn't giving the *Arcturus* guys a break."

The whistle blew for them to return to the goal line.

"Well," asked Roger, "do we freeze or don't we?"

"I don't want to. But majority always rules in this unit, Roger." Tom glanced at Astro. "How about it, Astro?"

"We can beat 'em fair and square. We play all out!" answered Astro.

Roger didn't say anything. He moved to one side and took his position for the dash down field.

The whistle blew again and the crowd roared as the two teams charged toward the ball. The cadets were eager to see if the *Arcturus* crew could tie the score or if the crew of the *Polaris* would increase its lead. But after a few moments of play, their cries of encouragement subsided into rumbles of discontent. In its eagerness to score, the *Arcturus* unit kept making errors and lost the ball constantly but the crew of the *Polaris* failed to capitalize. The second period ended with the score unchanged.

As he slumped to the ground for the rest period, Astro turned on Roger bitterly. "What's the idea, Manning? You're dogging it!"

"You play your game, Astro," replied Roger calmly, "I'll play mine."

"We're playing this game as a team, Roger," chimed in Tom heatedly. "You're kicking the ball all over the lot!"

"Yeah," added Astro. "In every direction except the goal!"

"I was never clear," defended Roger. "I didn't want to lose possession of the ball!"

"You sure didn't," said Tom. "You acted as if it was your best friend and you never wanted to be separated from it!"

"We said we didn't want to freeze this game, Roger, and we meant it!" Astro glowered at his unit-mate. "Next period you show us some action! If you don't want to score, feed it to us and we'll save you the trouble!"

But the third period was the same. While Tom and Astro dashed up and down the field, blocking out the members of the *Arcturus* crew to give Roger a clear shot, he simply nudged the ball back and forth between the side lines, ignoring his teammates' pleas to drive forward. As the whistle sounded for the end of the period, boos and catcalls from the grandstand filled the air.

Tom's face was an angry red as he faced Roger again on the side lines during the rest period.

"You hear that, Roger?" he growled, nodding his head toward the stands. "That's what they think of your smart playing!"

"What do I care?" replied the blond cadet arrogantly. "They're not playing this game! I am!"

"And we are too!" Astro's voice was a low rumble as he came up behind Manning. "If you don't give us a chance, so help me, I'll use your head for a ball!"

"If you're so interested in scoring, why don't you go after the ball yourselves then?" said Roger.

"Because we're too busy trying to be a team!" snapped Tom. "We're trying to clear shots for you!"

"Don't be so generous," sneered Roger.

"I'm warning you, Roger"—Astro glared at the arrogant cadet—"if you don't straighten out and fly right—"

McKenny's whistle from the far side lines suddenly sounded, interrupting the big cadet, and the three boys trooped back out on the field again. Again the air was filled with boos and shouts of derision and Tom's face flushed with shame.

This time, when McKenny's hand flashed downward, Tom streaked for the ball, instead of Schohari, his usual opponent. He measured his stride carefully and reached the ball in perfect kicking position.

He felt the satisfying thud against his foot, and saw the ball shoot out high in front of him and head for the goal line. It was a beautiful kick. But then, the ball suddenly sank, its flight altered by the action of the mercury. Running down field, Tom saw Swift and Allen meet the ball together. Allen blocked it with his chest and caromed it over to Swift. Swift let the ball drop to the ground, drawing his foot back to kick. But again, the mercury changed the ball's action, twisting it to one side and Swift's kick caught it on the side. Instead of the ball going down field, it veered to the left, in the path of Astro. Quickly getting his head under it, he shifted it to Roger, who streaked in and stopped it with his hip. But then, instead of passing ahead to Tom, who by now was down field and in the open, Roger prepared to kick for the goal himself.

Tom shouted a warning but it was too late. Schohari came rushing in behind him, and at running stride, met the ball squarely with his right foot. It sailed high in the air and over the *Polaris* goal line just as the whistle blew. The game was tied.

"That was some play, Manning," said Astro, when they were lined up waiting for the next period to begin.

"You asked for it," snapped Roger, "you were yapping at me to play, and now look what's happened!"

"Listen, you loudmouthed punk!" said Astro, advancing toward the smaller cadet, but just then the whistle blew and the three boys ran out onto the field.

The *Arcturus* crew swept down the field quickly, heading for the ball and seemingly ignoring the *Polaris* unit. But Schohari slipped and fell on the grass which gave Tom a clear shot at the ball. He caught it with the side of his boot and passed it toward Roger. But Allen, at full speed, came in and intercepted, sending the ball in a crazy succession of twists, turns and bounces. The crowd came to its feet as all six cadets made desperate attempts to clear the skittering ball with none of them so much as touching it. This was the part of mercuryball that pleased the spectator. Finally, Schohari managed to get a toe on it and he sent it down field, but Astro had moved out to play defense. He stopped the ball on his shoulder and dropped it to the ground. Steadying it there, he waited until Tom was in the clear and kicked it forty yards to the mid-field stripe.

The crowd came to its feet, sensing this final drive might mean victory for the *Polaris* crew. The boys of the *Arcturus* swarmed in—trying to keep Tom from scoring. With a tremendous burst of speed, Tom reached the ball ahead of Schohari, and with the strength of desperation, he slammed his foot against it. The whistle blew ending the game as the ball rose in an arc down the field and fell short of the goal by ten feet. There was a groan from the crowd.

But suddenly the ball, still reacting to the mercury inside, spun like a top, rolled sideways, and as if it were being blown by a breeze, rolled toward the goal line and stopped six inches inside the white chalk line.

There was a moment's pause as the crowd and the players, stunned by the play, grasped what had happened. Then swelling into a roar, there was one word chanted over and over—"*Polaris—Polaris—Polaris* . . ."

The *Polaris* unit had reached the finals of the Academy tournament.

* * * * *

During the intermission Charlie Wolcheck, unit commander of the *Capella* crew, walked over to the refreshment unit behind the grandstand where Steve Strong, Dr. Dale and Commander Walters were drinking Martian water and eating spaceburgers.

"Afternoon, Commander," saluted Wolcheck. "Hello, Joan, Steve. Looks as though your boys on the *Polaris* are going to meet their match this afternoon. I've got to admit they're good, but with Tony Richards feeding passes to Al Davison and with the blocking of Scott McAvoy—" The young officer broke off with a grin.

"I don't know, Charlie," Commander Walters said with a wink to Dr. Dale. "From the looks of Cadet Astro, if he ever gets his foot on the ball, your *Capella* unit will have to go after it with a jet boat."

"Why, Commander," replied Wolcheck, laughing good-naturedly, "Tony Richards is one of the finest booters I've ever seen. Saw him make a goal from the sixty-yard line from a standstill."

Steve Strong waved a Martian water pop bottle at young Wolcheck in a gesture of friendly derision.

"Did you happen to see the play in the first period?" he boasted. "Manning took a perfect pass from Astro and scored.

You're finished, Wolcheck, you and your *Capella* unit won't even come close."

"From what I hear and see, Manning seems to be a little sore that he can't make all the scores himself," grinned Wolcheck slyly. "He wants to be the whole show!"

Strong reddened and turned to put the empty bottle on the counter, using it as an excuse to hide his feelings from the commander and Joan. So Wolcheck had observed Manning's attitude and play on the field too.

Before Strong could reply, a bugle sounded from the field and the group of Solar Guard officers returned to their seats for the final game of the tournament between the *Capella* and the *Polaris* units.

Out on the field Mike made his usual speech about playing fair and gave the cadets the routine instructions of the game, reminding them that they were spacemen first, unit-members second, and individuals third and last. The six boys shook hands and jogged down the field to take up their positions.

"How about concentrating on the passes Richards is going to feed to Davison," Tom asked his unit-mates. "Never mind blocking out Richards and McAvoy."

"Yeah," agreed Astro, "play for the ball. Sounds good to me."

"How about it, Roger?" asked Tom.

"Just play the game," said Roger. And then added sarcastically, "And don't forget to give them every chance to score. Let's play fair and square, the way we did with the *Arcturus* unit."

"If you feel that way, Manning," answered Astro coldly, "you can quit right now! We'll handle the *Capella* guys ourselves!"

Before Roger could answer, McKenny blew the ready whistle and the three boys lined up along the white chalk line preparing for the dash to the waiting ball.

The cadets in the stands were hushed. McKenny's hand swept up and then quickly down as he blew the whistle. The crowd came to its feet, roaring, as Tom, five steps from his own goal line, tripped and fell headlong to the grass, putting him out of the first play. Astro and Roger charged down the field, with Astro reaching the ball first. He managed a good kick, but Richards, three feet away, took the ball squarely on his chest. The mercuryball fell to the ground, spun in a dizzy circle and with a gentle tap by Richards, rolled to Davison, who took it in stride and sent it soaring for a forty-five-yard goal.

The *Capella* unit had drawn first blood.

"Well, hot-shot," snarled Roger back on the starting line, "what happened to the big pass-stealing idea?"

"I tripped, Manning," said Tom through clenched teeth.

"Yeah! Tripped!" sneered Roger.

The whistle blew for the next goal.

Tom, with an amazing burst of speed, swept down the field, broke stride to bring him in perfect line with the ball and with a kick that seemed almost lazy, sent the ball from a dead standstill, fifty yards over the *Capella* goal before any of the remaining players were within five feet of it, and the score was tied.

The crowd sprang to its feet again and roared his name.

"That was terrific!" said Astro, slapping Tom on the back as they lined up again. "It looked as though you hardly kicked that ball at all."

"Yeah," muttered Roger, "you really made yourself the grandstand's delight!"

"What's that supposed to mean, Manning?" asked Astro.

"Superman Corbett probably burned himself out! Let's see him keep up that speed for the next ten minutes!"

The whistle blew for the next goal, and again the three boys moved forward to meet the onrushing *Capella* unit.

Richards blocked Astro with a twist of his body, and without stopping his forward motion, kicked the ball squarely toward the goal. It stopped ten feet short, took a dizzying spin and rolled away from the goal line. In a flash, the six boys were around the ball, blocking, shoving, and yelling instructions to each other while at the same time kicking at the unsteady ball. With each grazing kick, the ball went into even more maddening spins and gyrations.

At last Richards caught it with the side of his foot, flipped it to McAvoy who dropped back, and with twenty feet between him and the nearest *Polaris* member, calmly booted it over the goal. The whistle blew ending the first period, and the *Capella* unit led two to one.

During the next three periods, the *Capella* unit worked like a well-oiled machine. Richards passed to Davison or McAvoy, and when they were too well guarded, played brilliantly alone. The *Polaris* unit, on the other hand, appeared to be hopelessly outclassed. Tom and Astro fought like demons but Roger's lack of interest gave the *Capella* unit the edge in play. At the end of the fourth period, the *Capella* team led by three points, seven to four.

While the boys rested before the fifth and final period, Captain Strong, having watched the play with keen interest, realized that Roger was not playing up to his fullest capabilities. Suddenly he summoned a near-by Earthworm cadet, scribbled a message on a slip of paper and instructed the cadet to take it directly to Roger.

"Orders from the coach on the side lines?" asked Wolcheck as he noticed Strong's action.

"You might call it that, Charlie," answered Steve blandly.

On the field, the cadet messenger handed Roger the slip of paper, not mentioning that it was from Strong, and hurried back to the stands.

"Getting fan mail already?" asked Astro.

Roger ignored the comment and opened the slip of paper to read:

" . . . It might interest you to know that the winning team of the mercuryball finals is to be awarded a first prize of three days' liberty in Atom City . . ." There was no signature.

Roger stared up into the stands and searched vainly for some indication of the person who might have sent him the note. The crowd hushed as McKenny stepped forward for the starting of the last period.

"What was in the note, Roger?" asked Tom.

"The winning combination," smiled Roger lazily. "Get set for the fastest game of mercuryball you've ever played, Corbett! We've got to pull this mess out of the fire!"

Bewildered, Tom looked at Astro who merely shrugged his shoulders and took his place ready for the whistle. Roger tucked the note into his shorts and stepped up to the line.

"Listen, Corbett," said Roger, "every time Richards gets the ball, he kicks it to his left, and then McAvoy feints as if to get it, leaving Davison in the open. When you go to block Davison, you leave Richards in the clear. He just keeps the ball. He's scored three times that way!"

"Yeah," said Tom, "I noticed that, but there was nothing I could do about it, the way you've been playing."

"Kinda late in the game for any new ideas, Manning," growled Astro. "Just get the ball and pass it to me."

"That's my whole idea! Play back, Astro. Move like you're very tired, see? Then they'll forget about you and play three on two. You just be ready to kick and kick hard!"

"What's happened to you, Roger?" asked Tom. "What was in that note?"

Before Roger could answer, the whistle and the roar from the crowd signaled the beginning of the last period. The cadets raced down the field, Roger swerving to the left and making a feint at blocking Richards. He missed intentionally and allowed Richards to get the ball, who immediately passed to the left. McAvoy raced in on the ball, Tom made a move as if to block him, reversed, and startled the onrushing Richards with a perfect block. The ball was in the clear. Roger gave it a half kick and the ball landed two feet in front of Astro. The big cadet caught it perfectly on the first bounce and kicked it on a line across the goal, seventy yards away.

Up in the stands, Steve Strong smiled as he watched the score change on the board: "*Capella* seven—*Polaris* five!"

In rapid succession, the *Polaris* unit succeeded in intercepting the play of the *Capella* unit and rolling up two goals to an even score. Now, there were only fifty-five seconds left to play.

The cadets in the stands roared their approval of the gallant effort made by the three members of the *Polaris* crew. It had been a long time since mercuryball had been played with such deadly accuracy at Space Academy and everyone who attended the game was to remember for years to come the last play of the game.

McKenny blew the whistle again and the boys charged forward, but by now, aware of the sudden flash of unity on the part of the opposing team, the *Capella* unit fought desperately to salvage at least a tie.

Tom managed to block a kick by Richards, and the ball took a dizzy hop to the left, landing in front of Astro. He was in the clear. The stands were in an uproar as the cadets saw that the game was nearly over. Astro paused a split second, judged the ball and stepped forward to kick. But the ball spun away, just as Astro swung his leg. And at that instant, McAvoy came charging in from the left, only to be blocked by Roger. But the force of McAvoy's charge knocked Roger back into Astro. Instead of kicking the ball, Astro caught Roger on the side of the head. Roger fell to the ground and lay still. He was knocked cold. Astro lost his balance, twisted on one leg unsteadily, and then fell to the ground. When he tried to get up, he couldn't walk. He had twisted his ankle.

The *Capella* unit members stood still, confused and momentarily unable to take advantage of their opportunity. Without a moment's hesitation, Tom swept in and kicked the ball before his opponents realized what had happened. The ball drifted up in a high arc and landed with several bounces, stopping five feet from the goal.

Suddenly Richards, McAvoy and Davison came alive and charged after Tom, who was running for the ball as fast as his weary legs would carry him. He saw Richards pull up alongside of him, then pass him. Then Davison and McAvoy closed in on either side to block and give Richards a clear shot back down the field and a certain score.

Richards reached the ball, stopped and carefully lined up his kick, certain that his teammates could block out Tom. But the young cadet, in a last desperate spurt, outraced both McAvoy and Davison. Then, as Richards cocked his foot to kick, Tom jumped. With a mighty leaping dive, he sent his body hurtling headlong toward Richards just as he kicked. Tom's body crashed into the ball and Richards. The two boys went down in a heap but the ball caromed off his chest and rolled over the goal line.

The whistle blew ending the game.

In an instant, two thousand officers, cadets and enlisted men went wild as the ball rolled across the goal line.

The *Polaris* crew had won eight goals to seven!

From every corner of the field, the crowd cheered the cadets who had finished the game, had won it in the final seconds with two of them sprawled on the field unconscious and a third unable to stand on his feet.

Up in the stands, Captain Strong turned to Commander Walters. He found it hard to keep his eyes from filling up as he saluted briskly.

"Captain Strong reporting, sir, on the success of the *Polaris* unit to overcome their differences and become a fighting unit! And I mean *fight!*"

CHAPTER 11

"Atom City Express now arriving on track two!" The voice boomed over the loud-speaker system; and as the long, gleaming line of monorail cars eased to a stop with a soft hissing of brakes, the three cadets of the *Polaris* unit moved eagerly in that direction.

"Atom City, here we come," cried Astro.

"We and a lot of others with the same idea," said Tom. And, in fact, there were only a few civilians in the crowd pressing toward the car doors. Uniforms predominated—the blue of the cadets, enlisted men in scarlet, even a few in the black and gold uniforms which identified the officers of the Solar Guard.

"Personally," whispered Tom to his friends, "the first thing I want to do at Atom City is take a long walk—somewhere where I won't see a single uniform."

"As for me," drawled Roger, "I'm going to find a stereo studio where they're showing a Liddy Tamal feature. I'll sit down in a front-row seat and just watch that girl act for about six hours."

He turned to Astro. "And how about you?"

"Why . . . why . . . I'll string along with you, Roger," said the cadet from Venus. "It's been a long time since I've seen a—a—"

Tom and Roger laughed.

"A what?" teased Tom.

"A—a—girl," sputtered Astro, blushing.

"I don't believe it," said Roger in mock surprise. "I never—"

"Come on," interrupted Tom. "Time to get aboard."

They hurried across the platform and entered the sleek car. Inside they found seats together and sank into the luxurious chairs.

Astro sighed gently, stretched out his long legs and closed his eyes blissfully for a few moments.

"Don't wake me till we get started," he said.

"We already have," returned Tom. "Take a look."

Astro's eyes popped open. He glanced through the clear crystal glass at the rapidly moving landscape.

"These express jobs move on supercushioned ball bearings," explained Tom. "You can't even feel it when you pull out of the station."

"Blast my jets!" marveled Astro. "I'd sure like to take a look at the power unit on this baby."

"Even on a vacation, all this guy can think about is power!" grumbled Roger.

"How about building up our own power," suggested Tom. "It's a long haul to Atom City. Let's get a bite to eat."

"O.K. with me, spaceboy!" Astro grinned. "I could swallow a whole steer!"

"That's a great idea, cadet," said a voice from behind them.

It came from a gray-haired man, neatly dressed in the black one-piece stylon suit currently in fashion, and with a wide red sash around his waist.

"Beg pardon, sir," said Tom, "were you speaking to us?"

"I certainly was," replied the stranger. "I'm asking you to be my guests at dinner. And while I may not be able to buy your friend a whole steer, I'll gladly get him a piece of one."

"Hey," said Astro, "do you think he means it?"

"He seems to," replied Tom. He turned to the stranger. "Thanks very much, sir, but don't think Astro was just kidding about his appetite."

"I'm sure he wasn't." The gray-haired man smiled, and came over and stretched out his hand. "Then it's a deal," he said. "My name's Joe Bernard."

"Bernard!" exclaimed Roger. He paled and glanced quickly at his two friends, but they were too busy looking over their new friend to notice.

"Glad to know you, sir," said Tom. "I'm Tom Corbett. This is Astro, from Venus. And over here is—"

"Roger's my name," the third cadet said quickly. "Won't you sit down, sir?"

"No use wasting time," said Bernard. "Let's go right into the dining car." The cadets were in no mood to argue with him. They picked up the small microphones beside their chairs and sent food orders to the kitchen; and by the time they were seated in the dining car, their orders were ready on the table.

Mr. Bernard, with a twinkle in his eye, watched them enjoy their food. In particular, he watched Astro.

"I warned you, sir," whispered Tom, as the Venusian went to work on his second steak.

"I wouldn't have missed this for anything," said Bernard. He smiled, lit a cigar of fine Mercurian leaf tobacco and settled back comfortably.

"And now," he said, "let me explain why I was so anxious to have dinner with you. I'm in the import-export business. Ship to Mars, mostly. But all my life I've wanted to be a spaceman."

"Well, what was the trouble, Mr. Bernard?" asked Roger.

The man in black sighed. "Couldn't take the acceleration, boys. Bad heart. I send out more than five hundred cargoes a year, to all parts of the solar system; but myself, I've never been more than a mile off the surface of the earth."

"It sure must be disappointing—to want to blast off, and know that you can't," said Tom.

"I tried, once," said Bernard, with a rueful smile. "Yup! I tried." He gazed thoughtfully out the window.

"When I was your age, about twenty, I wanted to get into Space Academy worse than anybody I'd ever met." He paused. "Except for one person. A boyhood buddy of mine—named Kenneth—"

"Excuse me, sir," cut in Roger quickly, "but I think we'd better get back to our car. With this big liberty in front of us, we need a lot of rest."

"But, Roger!" exclaimed Tom.

Bernard smiled. "I understand, Roger. Sometimes I forget that I'm an old man. And when you've already tasted the excitement of space travel, talk like mine must seem rather dull." He stood up and faced the three cadets. "It's been very pleasant, Corbett, Astro, Roger. Now run along and get your rest. I'll just sit here for a while and watch the scenery."

"Thank you, sir," said Tom, "for the dinner—your company—and everything," he finished lamely.

There was a chorus of good-byes and the boys returned to their car. But there was little conversation now. Gradually, the lights in the cars dimmed to permit sleep. But Tom kept listening to the subdued click of the monorail—and kept wondering. Finally Roger, sleeping next to him, wakened for a moment.

"Roger," said Tom, "I want to ask you something."

"Wait'll the mornin'," mumbled Roger. "Wanta sleep."

"The way you acted with Bernard," Tom persisted. "You ate his dinner and then acted like he was poison. Why was that, Roger?"

The other sat bolt upright. "Listen," he said. "Listen!" Then he slumped back in his chair and closed his eyes. "Lemme sleep, Corbett. Lemme sleep, I tell you." He turned his back and in a moment was making sounds of deep slumber, but Tom felt sure that Roger was not asleep—that he was wide awake, with something seriously bothering him.

Tom leaned back and gazed out over the passing plains and up into the deep black of space. The Moon was full, large and round. He could distinguish *Mare Imbrium*, the largest of Luna's flat plains visible from Earth, where men had built the great metropolis of Luna City. Farther out in the deep blackness, he could see Mars, glowing like a pale ruby. Before long he would be up there again. Before long he would be blasting off in the *Polaris* with Astro and with Roger—

Roger! Why had he acted so strangely at dinner?

Tom remembered the night he saw Roger in Galaxy Hall alone at night, and the sudden flash on the field a few days before when they had won the mercuryball game. Was there some reason behind his companion's strange actions? In vain, Tom racked his brain to find the answer. There had to be some explanation. Yet what could it possibly be? He tossed and turned and worried and finally—comfortable as the monorail car was—he fell asleep from sheer exhaustion.

* * * * *

Atom City! Built of the clear crystal mined so cheaply on Titan, moon of Saturn, Atom City had risen from a barren North American wasteland to become a show place of the universe. Here was the center of all space communications—a proud city of giant crystal buildings. Here had been developed the first slidewalks, air cars, three-dimensional stereos and hundreds of other ideas for better living.

And here at Atom City was the seat of the great Solar Alliance, housed in a structure which covered a quarter of a mile at its base and which towered three thousand noble feet into the sky.

The three cadets stepped out of the monorail and walked across the platform to a waiting air car—jet-powered, shaped like a teardrop and with a clear crystal top.

"We want the best hotel in town," said Astro grandly to the driver.

"And get this speed bug outa here in a hurry," Roger told him. "There's a lot we want to do."

The driver couldn't help smiling at the three cadets so obviously enjoying their first leave.

"We've got three top hotels," he said. "One's as good as the other. They're the Earth, the Mars and the Venus."

"The Earth," voted Tom.

"The Mars," shouted Roger.

"The *Venus*!" roared Astro.

"All right," said the driver with a laugh, "make up your minds."

"Which of 'em is nearest the center of the city?" Tom asked.

"The Mars."

"Then blast off for Mars!" ordered Tom, and the air car shot away from the station and moved up into the stream of expressway traffic fifty feet above the ground.

As the little car sped along the broad avenue, Tom remembered how often, as a boy, he'd envied the Space Cadets who'd come to his home town of New Chicago on leave. Now here *he* was—in uniform, with a three-day pass, and all of Atom City to enjoy it in.

A few minutes later the air car stopped in front of the Mars Hotel. The cadets saw the entrance loom before them—a huge opening, with ornate glass and crystal in many different colors.

They walked across the high-ceilinged lobby toward the desk. All around them, the columns that supported the ceiling were made of the clearest crystal. Their feet sank into soft, lustrous deep-pile rugs made of Venusian jungle grass.

The boys advanced toward the huge circular reception desk where a pretty girl with red hair waited to greet them.

"May I help you?" she asked. She flashed a dazzling smile.

"You're a lucky girl," said Roger. "It just so happens you *can* help me. We'll have dinner together—just the two of us—and then we'll go to the stereos. After which we'll—"

The girl shook her head sadly. "I can see your friend's got a bad case of rocket shock," she said to Tom.

"That's right," Tom admitted. "But if you'll give us a triple room, we'll make sure he doesn't disturb anybody."

"Ah," said Roger, "go blow your jets!"

"I have a nice selection of rooms here on photo-slides if you'd care to look at them," the girl suggested.

"How many rooms in this hotel, Beautiful?" asked Roger.

"Nearly two thousand," answered the girl.

"And you have photo-slides of all two thousand?"

"Why, yes," answered the girl. "Why do you ask?"

"You and Astro go take a walk, Corbett," said Roger with a grin. "I'll select our quarters!"

"You mean," asked the girl, a little flustered, "you want to look at all the slides?"

"Sure thing, Lovely!" said Roger with a lazy smile.

"But—but that would take three hours!"

"Exactly my idea!" said Roger.

"Just give us a nice room, Miss," said Tom, cutting in. "And please excuse Manning. He's so smart, he gets a little dizzy now and then. Have to take him over to a corner and revive him." He glanced at Astro, who picked Roger up in his arms and walked away with him as though he were a baby.

"Come on, you space Romeo!" said Astro.

"Hey—ouch—hey—lemme go, ya big ape. You're killing your best friend!" Roger twisted around in Astro's viselike grasp, to no avail.

"Space fever," explained Tom. "He'll be O.K. soon."

"I think I understand," said the girl with a nervous smile.

She handed Tom a small flashlight. "Here's your photoelectric light key for room 2305 F. That's on the two hundred thirtieth floor."

Tom took the light key and turned toward the slidestairs where Astro was holding Roger firmly, despite his frantic squirming.

"Hey, Tom," cried Roger, "tell this Venusian ape to let me go!"

"Promise to behave yourself?" asked Tom.

"We came here to have fun, didn't we?" demanded Roger.

"That doesn't mean getting thrown out of the hotel because you've got to make passes at every beautiful girl."

"What's the matter with beautiful girls?" growled Roger. "They're official equipment, like a radar scanner. You can't get along without them!"

Tom and Astro looked at each other and burst out laughing.

"Come on, you jerk," said Astro, "let's get washed up. I wanta take a walk and get something to eat. I'm hungry again!"

An hour later, showered and dressed in fresh uniforms, the *Polaris* crew began a tour of the city. They went to the zoo and saw dinosaurs, a tyrannosaurus, and many other monsters extinct on Earth millions of years ago, but still breeding in the jungles of Tara. They visited the council chamber of the Solar Alliance where delegates from the major planets and from the larger satellites, such as Titan of Saturn, Ganymede of Jupiter, and Luna of Earth made the laws for the tri-planetary league. The boys walked through the long halls of the Alliance building, looking at the great documents which had unified the solar system.

They reverently inspected original documents of the Universal Bill of Rights and the Solar Constitution, which guaranteed basic freedoms of speech, press, religion, peaceful assembly and representative government. And even brash, irrepressible Roger Manning was awestruck as they tiptoed into the great Chamber of the Galactic Court, where the supreme judicial body of the entire universe sat in solemn dignity.

Later, the boys visited the Plaza de Olympia—a huge fountain, filled with water taken from the Martian Canals, the lakes of Venus and the oceans of Earth, and ringed by a hundred large statues, each one symbolizing a step in mankind's march through space.

But then, for the Space Cadets, came the greatest thrill of all—a trip through the mighty Hall of Science, at once a museum of past progress and a laboratory for the development of future wonders.

Thousands of experiments were being conducted within this crystal palace, and as Space Cadets, the boys were allowed to witness a few of them. They watched a project which sought to harness the solar rays more effectively; another which aimed to create a new type of fertilizer for Mars, so people of that planet would be able to grow their own food in their arid deserts instead of importing it all from other worlds. Other scientists were trying to adapt Venusian jungle plants to grow on other planets with a low oxygen supply; while still others, in the medical field, sought for a universal antibody to combat all diseases.

Evening finally came and with it time for fun and entertainment. Tired and leg weary, the cadets stepped on a slidewalk and allowed themselves to be carried to a huge restaurant in the heart of Atom City.

"Food," exulted Astro as the crystal doors swung open before them. "Smell it! Real, honest-to-gosh food!" He rushed for a table.

"Hold it, Astro," shouted Tom. "Take it easy."

"Yeah," added Roger. "It's been five hours since your last meal—not five weeks!"

"Meal!" snorted the Venusian cadet. "Call four spaceburgers a meal? And anyway, it's been six hours, not five."

Laughing, Tom and Roger followed their friend inside. Luckily, they found a table not far from the door, where Astro grabbed the microphone and ordered his usual tremendous dinner.

The three boys ate hungrily as course after course appeared on the middle of the table, via the direct shaft from the kitchen. So absorbed was Manning that he did not notice the approach of a tall dark young man of about his own age, dressed in the red-brown uniform of the Passenger Space Service. But the young man, who wore a captain's high-billed hat, suddenly caught sight of Roger.

"Manning," he called, "what brings you here?"

"Al James!" cried Roger and quickly got up to shake hands. "Of all the guys in the universe to show up! Sit down and have a bite with us."

The space skipper sat down. Roger introduced him to Tom and Astro. There was a round of small talk.

"Whatever made you become a Space Cadet, Roger?" asked James finally.

"Oh, you know how it is," said Roger. "You can get used to anything."

Astro almost choked on a mouthful of food. He shot a glance at Tom, who shook his head as though warning him not to speak.

James grinned broadly. "I remember how you used to talk back home. The Space Cadets were a bunch of tin soldiers trying to feel important. The Academy was a lot of space gas. I guess, now, you've changed your mind."

"Maybe I have," said Roger. He glanced uneasily at his two friends, but they pretended to be busy eating. "Maybe I have." Roger's eyes narrowed, his voice became a lazy drawl. "At that it's better'n being a man in a monkey suit, with nothing to do but impress the passengers and order around the crew."

"Wait a minute," said James. "What kind of a crack is that?"

"No crack at all. Just the way I feel about you passenger gents who don't know a rocket tube from a ray-gun nozzle."

"Look, Manning," returned James. "No need to get sore, just because you couldn't do any better than the Space Cadets."

"Blast off," shouted Roger, "before I fuse your jets."

Tom spoke up. "I think you'd better go, Captain."

"I've got six men outside," sneered the other. "I'll go when I'm ready."

"You're ready now," spoke up Astro. He stood up to his full height. "We don't want any trouble," the cadet from Venus said, "but we're not braking our jets to get away from it, either."

James took a good look at Astro's powerful frame. Without another word he walked away.

Tom shook his head. "That pal of yours is a real Space Cadet fan, isn't he, Roger?"

"Yeah," said Astro. "Just like Manning is himself."

"Look," said Roger. "Look, you guys—" He hesitated, as though intending to say something more, but then he turned back to his dinner. "Go on—finish your food," he growled. He bent over his plate and ate without lifting his eyes. And not another word was spoken at the table until a young man approached, carrying a portable televiewer screen.

"Pardon me," he said. "Is one of you Cadet Tom Corbett?"

"Why—I am," acknowledged Tom.

"There's a call for you. Seems they've been trying to reach you all over Atom City." He placed the televiewer screen on the table, plugged it into a floor socket and set the dials.

"Hope's there's nothing wrong at home," said Tom to his friends. "My last letter from Mom said Billy was messing around with a portable atom reactor and she was afraid he might blow himself up."

A picture began to take shape on the screen. "Migosh," said Astro. "It's Captain Strong."

"It certainly is," said the captain's image. "Having dinner, eh, boys? Ummmm—those baked shrimps look good."

"They're terrific," said Astro. "Wish you were here."

"Wish you could stay there," said Captain Strong.

"Oh, no!" moaned Astro. "Don't tell me!"

"Sorry, boys," came the voice from the teleceiver. "But that's it. You've got to return to the Academy immediately. The whole cadet corps has been ordered into space for special maneuvers. We blast off tomorrow morning at six hundred."

"But, sir," objected Tom, "we can't get a monorail until morning!"

"This is an official order, Corbett. So you have priority over all civilian transportation." The Solar Guard captain smiled. "I've tied up a whole bank of teleceivers in Atom City searching for you. Get back to Space Academy fast—commandeer an air car if you must, but be here by six hundred hours!" The captain waved a cheery good-bye and the screen went dark.

"Space maneuvers," breathed Astro. "The real thing."

"Yeah," agreed Tom. "Here we go!"

"Our first hop into deep space!" said Roger. "Let's get out of here!"

CHAPTER 12

"The following ships in Squadron A will blast off immediately," roared Commander Walters over the teleceiver. He looked up alertly from a chart before him in the Academy spaceport control tower. He began to name the ships. "*Capella*, orbital tangent—09834, *Arcturus*, orbital tangent—09835, *Centauri*, orbital tangent—09836, *Polaris*, orbital tangent—09837!"

Aboard the space cruiser *Polaris*, Tom Corbett turned away from the control board. "That's us, sir," he said to Captain Strong.

"Very well, Corbett." The Solar Guard captain walked to the ship's intercom and flipped on the switch.

"Astro, Roger, stand by!"

Astro and Roger reported in. Strong began to speak. "The cadet corps has been divided into squadrons of four ships each. We are command ship of Squadron A. When we reach free-fall space, we are to proceed as a group until eight hundred hours, when we are to open sealed orders. Each of the other seven squadrons will open their orders at the same time. Two of the squadrons will then act as invaders while the remaining six will be the defending fleet. It will be the invaders' job to reach their objective and the defenders' job to stop them."

"Spaceport control to rocket cruiser *Polaris*, your orbit has been cleared for blast-off . . ." The voice of Commander Walters interrupted Strong in his instructions and he turned back to Tom.

"Take over, Corbett."

Tom turned to the teleceiver. "Rocket cruiser *Polaris* to spaceport control."

". . . Blast off minus two—six hundred forty-eight . . ."

"I read you clear," said Tom. He clicked off the teleceiver and turned back to the intercom. "Stand by to raise ship! Control deck to radar deck. Do we have clear trajectory forward and up, Roger?"

"All clear forward and up," replied Roger.

"Control deck to power deck... energize the cooling pumps!"

"Cooling pumps, aye," came from Astro.

The giant ship began to shudder as the mighty pumps on the power deck started their build.

Tom strapped himself into the pilot's seat and began checking the dials in front of him. Satisfied, he fastened his eyes on the sweep hand of the time clock. Above his head, the teleceiver screen brought him a clear picture of the Academy spaceport. He watched the giant cruisers take to the air one by one and rocket into the vastness of space.

The clock hand reached the ten-second mark.

"Stand by to raise ship!" Tom called into the intercom. The red hand moved steadily, inexorably. Tom reached for the master switch.

"Blast off minus—five—four—three—two—one—*zero!*"

Tom threw the switch.

The great ship hovered above the ground for a few moments. Then it heaved itself skyward, faster and ever faster, pushing the Earthmen deep into their acceleration cushions.

Reaching free-fall space, Tom flipped on the artificial-gravity generator. He felt its pull on his body, quickly checked all the instruments and turned to Captain Strong.

"Ship space-borne at six hundred fifty-three, sir."

"Very well, Corbett," replied Strong. "Check in with the *Arcturus*, *Capella* and the *Centauri*, form up on one another and assume a course that will bring you back over Academy spaceport at eight hundred hours, when we will open orders."

"Yes, sir," said Tom, turning back eagerly to the control board.

For nearly two hours the four rocket ships of Squadron A moved through space in a perfect arc, shaping up for the 0800 deadline. Strong made use of the time to check a new astrogation prism perfected by Dr. Dale for use at hyperspace speeds. Tom rechecked his instruments, then prepared hot tea and sandwiches in the galley for his shipmates.

"This is what I call service," said Astro. He stood stripped to the waist, a wide leather belt studded with assorted wrenches of various shapes and sizes strapped around his hips. In one hand he carried a wad of waste cotton with which he continually polished the surfaces of the atomic motors, while his eyes constantly searched the many gauges in front of him for the slightest sign of engine failure.

"Never mind bringing anything up to Manning. I'll eat his share."

Astro had deliberately turned the intercom on so Roger on the radar deck might hear. The response from that corner was immediate and emphatic.

"Listen, you rocket-headed grease monkey," yelled Roger. "If you so much as smell that grub, I'll come down and feed you into the reactant chamber!"

Tom smiled at Astro and turned to the ladder leading up from the power deck. Passing through the control deck on the way to the radar bridge, he glanced at the clock. It was ten minutes to eight.

"Only one thing I'm worried about, Corbett," said Roger through a mouthful of sandwich.

"What's that?" asked Tom.

"Collision!" said Roger. "Some of these space-happy cadets might get excited, and I for one don't want to wind up as a flash in Earth's atmosphere!"

"Why, you have radar, to see anything that goes on."

"Oh, sure," said Roger, "I can keep this wagon outa their way, but will they stay outa mine? Why my father told me once—" Roger choked on his food and turned away to the radar screen.

"Well," said Tom after a moment, "what *did* your father tell you?"

"Ah—nothing—not important. But I've got to get a cross-fix on Regulus before we start our little games."

Tom looked puzzled. Here was another of Roger's quick changes of attitude. What was it all about? But there was work to do, so Tom shrugged his shoulders and returned to the control deck. He couldn't forget what Roger had said about a collision, though.

"Excuse me, Captain," said Tom, "but have there been any serious collisions in space between ships?"

"Sure have, Tom," replied Strong. "About twenty years ago, maybe less, there was a whole wave of them. That was before we developed superrebound pulse radar. The ships were faster than the radar at close range."

Strong paused. "Why do you ask?"

Before Tom could answer, there was a sharp warning from the captain.

"Eight o'clock, Corbett!"

Tom ripped open the envelope containing the sealed orders. "Congratulations," he read. "You are in command of the defenders. You have under your command, Squadrons A—B—C—D—E—F. Squadrons G and H are your enemies, and at this moment are on their way to attack Luna City. It is your job to protect it and destroy the enemy fleet. Spaceman's luck! Walters, Commander Space Academy, Senior Officer Solar Guard."

"Roger," yelled Tom, "we've been selected as flagship for the defenders! Get me a course to Luna City!"

"Good for us, spaceboy. I'll give you that course in a jiffy!"

" . . . *Capella* to *Polaris*—am standing by for your orders . . ." Tony Richards' voice crackled over the teleceiver. One by one the twenty-three ships that made up the defender's fleet checked in for orders.

"Astro," shouted Tom, "stand by for maneuver—and be prepared to give me every ounce of thrust you can get!"

"Ready, willing and able, Tom," replied Astro. "Just be sure those other space jockeys can keep up with me, that's all!"

Tom turned to Captain Strong.

"What do you think of approaching—"

Strong cut him off. "Corbett, you are in complete command. Take over—you're losing time talking to me!"

"Yes, sir!" said Tom. He turned back to the control board, his face flushed with excitement. Twenty-four ships to maneuver and the responsibility all his own. Via a chart projected on a screen, he studied various approaches to the Moon and Luna City. What would he do if he were in command of the invading fleet? He noticed the Moon was nearing a point where it would be in eclipse on Luna City itself. He studied the chart further, made several notations and turned to the teleceiver.

"Attention—attention—flagship *Polaris* to Squadrons B and C—proceed to chart seven—sectors eight and nine. You will patrol those sectors. Attention Squadrons D and F—proceed to Luna City at emergency space speed, hover at one hundred thousand feet above Luna City spaceport and wait for further orders. Attention, ships three and four of Squadron F—you will proceed to chart six—sectors sixty-eight through seventy-five.

"Attention Squadrons D and F—proceed to Luna City"

Cut all rockets and remain there until further orders. The remainder of Squadron F—ships one and two—will join Squadron A. Squadron A will stand by for further orders." Tom glanced at the clock and punched the intercom button.

"Have you got that course, Roger?"

"Three degrees on the starboard rockets, seventy-eight degrees on the up-plane of the ecliptic will put you at the corner of Luna Drive and Moonset Land in the heart of Luna City, spaceboy!" answered Roger.

"Get that, Astro?" asked Tom on the intercom.

"All set," replied Astro.

"Attention all ships in Squadron A—this is flagship—code name Starlight—am changing course. Stand by to form up on me!"

Tom turned back to the intercom.

"Power deck, execute!"

At more than five thousand miles an hour, the *Polaris* hurtled toward its destination. One by one the remaining ships moved alongside until all six had their needlelike noses pointed toward the pale satellite of the Moon.

"I'd like to know what your plans are, Tom," said Strong, when the long haul toward the Moon had settled down to a routine. "Just idle curiosity, nothing more. You don't have to tell me if you don't want to."

"Golly, yes," said Tom, "I'd be very grateful for your opinion."

"Well, let's have it," said the captain. "But as for my opinion—I'll listen, but I won't say anything."

Tom grinned sheepishly.

"Well," he began, "if I were in command of the invading fleet, I would strike in force—I'd have to, to do damage with only eight ships. There are three possible approaches to Luna City. One is from the Earth side, using the eclipse corridor of darkness as protection. To meet that, I've stationed two ships at different levels and distances in that corridor so that it would be impossible for an invasion to pass unnoticed."

"You mean, you'd be willing to give up two ships to the invader to have him betray his position. Is that right?"

"Yes, sir. But I've also sent Squadrons B and C to sectors eight and nine on chart seven. So I have a roving squadron to go to their aid, should the invader strike there. And on the other hand, should he manage to get through my outer defense, I have Squadrons D and E over Luna City itself as an inner defense. As for Squadron A, we'll try to engage the enemy first and maybe weaken him; at least reduce the full force of his attack. And then have Squadrons B, C, D and E finish him off, by attack from three different points."

Strong nodded silently. The young cadet was shaping up a defensive strategy with great skill. If he could only follow through on his plans, the invaders of Luna City wouldn't have much chance of success—even if willing to take heavy losses.

Roger's voice came on. "Got a report for you, Tom. From command ship, Squadron B. They've sighted the invaders and are advancing to meet them."

Tom checked his charts and turned to the intercom.

"Send them this message, Roger," he said. "From Starlight, to command ship, Squadrons B and C—approach enemy ships from position of chart nineteen, sections one through ten."

"Right!" said Roger.

Strong smiled. Tom was driving his heaviest force between the invading fleet and its objective—forcing the aggressors into a trap.

Tom gave more crisp orders to his squadrons. He asked Roger for an estimated range, and then, rechecking his position, turned again to the intercom.

"Astro, how much could you get out of this baby by opening the by-pass between the cooling pumps and the reactant chamber? That'd mean feeding the stuff into the motors only half cooled."

Strong turned, started to speak, then clamped his lips together.

"Another quarter space speed, roughly," replied Astro, "about fifteen hundred miles more an hour. Do you want me to do that?"

"No, not now," replied Tom. "Just wanted to know what I could depend on, if I get stuck."

"O.K.," said Astro. "Let me know!"

"Why use emergency speed, Corbett?" asked Strong. "You seem to have your enemy right where you want him now."

"Yes, sir," replied Tom. "And the enemy knows I have him. He can't possibly attack Luna City now. But he can still run away. He can make his escape by this one route."

Tom walked to the chart and ran his finger on a line away from the invader's position into the asteroid belt.

"I don't want him to get away," Tom explained. "And with the extra speed, we can cut him off, force him to turn into a position where the remainder of my fleet would finish him off."

"You'll do this with just the *Polaris*?"

"Oh, no, sir," said Tom. "I'd use the *Arcturus*, *Capella* and the *Centauri*, as well."

"Are you sure those other ships can equal your speed?"

"They've got exactly the same type engines as we have here on the *Polaris*, sir. I'm sure they could—and with perfect safety."

Strong hesitated a moment, started to ask a question, then stopped and walked to the chart screen. He checked the figures. He checked them four times, then turned to Tom with a grin and an outstretched hand.

"I've got to offer my congratulations, Tom. This maneuver would wipe them out. And I've got a notion that you'd come off without the loss of a single ship, plus, and it is a big plus, keeping the invaders more than fifty thousand miles away from their objective!"

The captain turned to the teleceiver. "Rocket cruiser *Polaris* to control tower at Space Academy—"

There was a crackle of static and then the deep voice of Commander Walters boomed from the speaker.

"Spaceport control to *Polaris*. Come in, Steve."

In a few brief sentences, Strong outlined Tom's plan of action to the Academy commander. The commander's face on the teleceiver widened into a grin, then broke out in a hearty laugh.

"What's that, sir?" asked Captain Strong.

"Very simple, Steve. All of us—all the Academy top brass—develop a foolproof test for cadet maneuvers. And then your young Corbett makes us look like amateurs."

"But didn't you expect one side or the other to win?" asked Strong.

"Of course, but not like this. We've been expecting a couple of days of maneuver, with both sides making plenty of mistakes that we could call them on. But here Corbett wraps the whole thing up before we can get our pencils sharpened."

"Better stuff cotton in Corbett's ears before he hears all this," rasped Roger Manning over the intercom. "Or his head'll be too big to go through the hatch."

"Quiet, Manning," came Astro's voice from the power deck. "Your mouth alone is bigger than Tom's head'll ever be."

"Look, you Venusian ape—" began Roger, but Commander Walters' voice boomed out again. His face on the teleceiver screen was serious now.

"Attention! Attention all units! The battle has been fought and won on the chart screen of the rocket cruiser *Polaris*. The Luna City attack has been repelled and the invading fleet wiped out. All units and ships will return to Space Academy at once. Congratulations to all and end transmission."

The commander's face faded from the screen. Captain Strong turned to Tom. "Good work," he said.

He was interrupted by a crackle of static from the teleceiver. A face suddenly appeared on the screen—a man's face, frightened and tense.

"S O S." The voice rang out through the control deck.

"This is an S O S. Space passenger ship *Lady Venus* requests assistance immediately. Position is sector two, chart one hundred three. Emergency. We must have—"

The screen went blank, the voice stopped as though cut off by a knife. Strong frantically worked the teleceiver dials to re-establish contact.

"*Polaris* to *Lady Venus*," he called. "Come in *Lady Venus*. Rocket cruiser *Polaris* calling *Lady Venus*. Come in! Come in!"

There was no answer. The passenger ship's instruments had gone dead.

CHAPTER 13

"*Polaris* to Commander Walters at Space Academy—Come in, Commander Walters!" Captain Strong's voice was urgent in the teleceiver.

"Just worked up an assumed position on the *Lady Venus*," said Roger over the intercom. "I think she's bearing about seventeen degrees to port of us, and about one-twenty-eight on the downplane of the ecliptic."

"O.K., Roger," said Tom. "Captain Strong's trying to reach Commander Walters now." He made a quick mental calculation. "Golly, Roger—if you've figured it right, we're closer to the *Lady Venus* than anyone else!"

The teleceiver audio crackled.

"Commander Walters at Space Academy to Captain Strong on the *Polaris*. Come in, Steve!"

"Commander!" Strong's voice sounded relieved. "Did you get that emergency from the *Lady Venus*—the S O S?"

"Yes, we did, Steve," said the commander. "How far away from her are you?"

Without a word, Tom handed Strong the position that Roger had computed. Strong relayed the information to the commander.

"If you're that close, go to her aid in the *Polaris*. You're nearer than any Solar Guard patrol ship and you can do just as much."

"Right, sir," replied Steve. "I'll report as soon as I get any news. End transmission!"

"Spaceman's luck, end transmission!" said the commander.

"Have you got a course for us, Roger?" asked Strong.

"Yes, sir!"

"Then let's get out of here. I have a feeling there's something more than just the usual emergency attached to that S O S from the *Lady Venus*."

In twenty seconds the mighty cruiser was blasting through space to the aid of the stricken passenger ship.

"Better get the emergency equipment ready, Tom," said Strong. "Space suits for the four of us and every spare space suit you have on the ship. Never can tell what we might run into. Also the first-aid surgical kit and every spare oxygen bottle. Oh, yeah, and have Astro get both jet boats ready to blast off immediately. I'll keep trying to pick them up again on the teleceiver."

"Yes, sir," replied Tom sharply.

"What's going on up there?" asked Astro, when Tom had relayed the orders from Captain Strong. Tom quickly told him of the emergency signal from the *Lady Venus*.

"*Lady—Venus—*" said the big cadet, rolling the name on his tongue, "I know her. She's one of the Martian City—Venusport jobs—an old-timer. Converted from a chemical burner to atomic reaction about three years ago!"

"Any ideas what the trouble might be?" asked Tom.

"I don't know," replied Astro. "There are a hundred and fifty things that could go wrong—even on this wagon and she's brand new. But I wouldn't be surprised if it was on the power deck!"

"And what makes you think so?" asked Tom.

"I knew a spaceman once that was on a converted tub just like the *Lady Venus* and he had trouble with the reaction chamber."

"Wow!" exclaimed Tom. "Let's hope it isn't that now!"

"You can say that again," said Astro grimly. "When this stuff gets out of control, there's very little you can do with it, except leave it alone and pile out!"

The *Polaris*, rocketing through space at full space speed, plunged like a silver bullet through the vastness of the black void, heading for what Strong hoped to be the *Lady Venus*. Tom prepared the emergency equipment, doubling all the reserves on the oxygen bottles by refilling the empties he found on the ship and making sure that all space suits were in perfect working order. Then he opened the emergency surgical kit and began the laborious task of examining every vial and drug in the kit to acquaint himself with what there was to work with just in case. He brought all the stores of jelly out for radiation burns and finally opened a bottle of special sterilization liquid with which to wipe all the instruments and vials clean. He checked the contents of the kit once more, and, satisfied that everything was as ready as he could make it, he went up to the control deck.

"Any other message from them yet, sir?" asked Tom.

"Nothing yet," answered Strong. "If I could pick them up on the teleceiver, maybe they could tell us what the trouble is and then we could more or less be prepared to help them." He bent over the teleceiver screen and added grimly, "If there is anything left to help!"

"Radar deck to control deck!" Roger's voice was tense. "I think I've picked them up on the radar scanner, Captain Strong!"

"Relay it down here to control-deck scanner, Manning," ordered Strong.

"Ummmh!" murmured the captain when the screen began to glow. "I'm pretty sure that's her. Here's that assumed position Roger worked up, Tom. Check it against this one here on the scanner."

Tom quickly computed the position of the object on the scanner and compared it to the position Roger had given them previously.

"If Roger's positioning was correct, sir," said Tom, "then that's the *Lady Venus*. They both check out perfectly!"

Strong, bent over the radar scanner, didn't answer. Finally he turned around and flipped off the scanner. "That's her," he announced. "Congratulations, Roger. You hit it right on the nose!"

"How shall we approach her, sir?" asked Tom.

"We'd better wait until she sends up her flares."

"You mean the identification flares for safety factors?"

"That's right," replied Strong. "A white flare means it's all right to come alongside and couple air locks. A red one means to stand off and wait for instructions." Strong turned to the intercom.

"Control deck to power deck. Reduce thrust to one quarter space speed!"

"Power deck, aye," answered Astro.

"We'll wait until we're about two miles away from her and then use our braking jets in the bow of the ship to bring us within a few thousand feet of her," commented Strong.

"Yes, sir," said Tom.

"Work up an estimated range, Roger," said Strong, "and give me a distance on our approach."

"Aye, aye, sir," Roger replied. "Objective four miles away now, sir."

"When we hit three miles," said Strong to Tom, "have Astro stand by the forward braking jets."

"Aye, sir," said Tom.

"Three-and-a-half miles," said Roger a few moments later. "Closing in fast. *Lady Venus* looks like a dead ship."

"That could only mean one thing," said Strong bitterly. "There has been a power-deck failure of some sort."

"Three miles to objective, sir," reported Roger. "I think I can pick her up on the teleceiver now, but only one way, from us to her."

"All right," said Strong, "see what you can do."

In a few moments the teleceiver screen glowed and then the silver outline of the *Lady Venus* appeared on the screen.

"I don't see any damage to her hull," said Strong half to himself. "So if it was an explosion, it wasn't a bad one."

"Yes, sir," said Tom. "Shall I stand by with the flares?"

"Better send up a yellow identification flare, identifying us as the Solar Guard. Let them know who we are!"

Tom turned to the yellow button on his left and pressed it. Immediately a white flash resembling a meteor appeared on the teleceiver screen.

"There should be an answer soon," said Strong.

"Three thousand yards to objective," reported Roger.

"Fire braking rockets one half," ordered Strong.

Tom relayed the order to Astro and made the necessary adjustments on the control panel.

"Stern drive rockets out," ordered Strong.

Once again Tom relayed the message to Astro and turned to the control board.

"Cut all rockets!" ordered Strong sharply.

The great ship, slowed by the force of the braking rockets, became motionless in space a bare five hundred yards from the *Lady Venus*.

"They should be sending up their safety-factor flare soon," said Strong. "Keep trying to raise them on the teleceiver, Roger."

Strong was peering through a crystal port directly at the ship hanging dead in space opposite them. There wasn't any sign of life. Tom stepped to the side of Steve Strong and looked out at the crippled passenger ship.

"Why don't we go aboard, sir?" asked Tom.

"We'll wait a little longer for the flare. If we don't get it soon—"

"There it is, sir!" shouted Tom at Strong's side.

From the flare port near the nose of the commercial ship, a ball of fire streaked out.

"Red!" said Strong grimly, "That means we can't go alongside. We'll have to use jet boats."

"Captain Strong," shouted Roger from the radar deck, "they're signaling us with a small light from the upper port on the starboard side!"

"Can you read it?" asked Strong quickly.

"I think so, sir. They're using standard space code, but the light is very dim."

"What do they say?"

"... reaction ... chamber—" said Roger slowly as he read the blinking light, "... radiation ... leaking around ... baffle ... all ... safe ..." Roger stopped. "That's all, sir. I couldn't get the rest of it."

Strong turned to the intercom. "Astro, get the jet boats ready to blast off immediately. Roger, send this message. 'Am coming aboard. Stand by to receive me on your number-one starboard jet-boat catapult deck, signed, Strong, Captain, Solar Guard.'"

"Yes, sir!" replied Roger.

"Get into your space suit, Tom, and give Astro a hand with the jet boats. I have to get a message back to Space Academy and tell them to send out help right away."

"Aye, sir," said Tom.

"Roger," said Strong, "stand by to record this message for the teleceiver in case Space Academy should call our circuit while we're off the ship."

"All set, sir," came the reply from the radar deck.

"O.K.—here goes—Captain Steve Strong—Solar Guard—am boarding passenger ship *Lady Venus*. Secondary communications signal message received indicates it is power-deck failure. Am taking cadets Corbett, Manning and Astro and boarding same at"—he paused and glanced at the clock—"thirteen hundred fifty one hours!"

"That all, sir?" asked Roger.

"That's it. Get that set on the open circuit for any one calling us, then climb into your space suit!"

In a matter of minutes, the four spacemen of the *Polaris* crew were making last-minute adjustments on their space suits. Astro picked up his heavy belt of tools and strapped them around his waist.

"What's that for, Astro?" asked Strong. "They'll have tools aboard the ship if we need them."

"If that lead baffle in the reaction chamber has worked loose, sir, the odds are ten to one that the control chamber is flooded with radiation. And if it is, the tools are probably so hot you couldn't use them."

"That's good thinking, Astro," complimented Strong. He turned to Tom and Roger and checked their suits and the oxygen supply and feeder valves on their backs. He then turned his back while Tom checked his, and Roger adjusted Astro's.

"All right, turn on your communicators and test them," ordered Strong.

One by one the boys flipped on the switch of the portable spacephones in their fish-bowl helmets and spoke to each other. Strong indicated that he was satisfied and turned toward the jet-boat catapult deck, the three boys following him in single file.

"Astro, you and Roger take number-one boat," said Strong. "Tom and I will take number two." His voice had a harsh metallic tone through the headset spacephones.

Roger hurried along with Astro to the number-one boat and climbed inside.

"Jet boat has its own oxygen system," said Astro to Roger. "Better make use of it while we're in here and save our suits' supplies."

"Good idea," said Roger. He locked the clear plastic airtight covering of the jet boat and began flicking at the control buttons.

"Strap in, you Venusian hick. Here we go!" Roger shoved a lever at his side, making the jet-boat deck airtight from the rest of the *Polaris*, and then, by pressing a button on the simple control board, a section of the *Polaris'* hull slipped back, exposing them to empty space.

The controls of a jet boat were simplicity itself. A half-moon wheel for guiding, up, down and either side, and two pedals on the floor, one for going and one for stopping. Roger stepped on the "Go" pedal and the small ship flashed out into the darkness of space.

Almost immediately on the opposite side of the *Polaris*, Captain Strong and Tom in the second boat shot away from the rocket cruiser and both boats headed for the stricken spaceship.

CHAPTER 14

The hatch clanked shut behind them. Inside the huge air lock of the *Lady Venus*, Tom, Roger, Astro and Captain Strong waited for the oxygen to equal the pressure in their space suits before removing their fish-bowl space helmets.

"O.K., sir," said Tom, "pressure's equal."

Strong stepped to the hatch leading to the inside of the ship and pushed hard. It slid to one side.

"How many jet boats do you have?" was the first thing Strong heard as he stepped through the door to the interior of the passenger ship.

"Al James!" cried Manning. "So this is your tub?"

The startled young skipper, whom Tom, Roger and Astro had met in Atom City, turned to face the blond-headed cadet.

"Manning!" he gasped.

"What's your trouble, skipper?" asked Strong of the young spaceship captain.

Before James could answer there was a sudden clamor from beyond the next hatch leading to the main passenger cabin. Suddenly the hatch was jerked open and a group of frightened men and women poured through. The first to reach Strong, a short fat man with a moonface and wearing glasses, began to jabber hysterically, while clinging to Strong's arm.

"Sir, this ship is going to blow up any moment. You've got to save us!" He turned to face Al James. "And he refused to allow us to escape in the jet boats!" He pointed an accusing finger at the young skipper as the other passengers loudly backed him up.

"Just a moment," snapped Strong. "There's a Solar Guard rocket cruiser only five hundred yards away, so take it easy and don't get hysterical. No one is going to get hurt if you keep calm and obey orders!" He turned to James. "What's the trouble, skipper?"

"It's the reaction chamber. The lead baffle around the chamber worked loose and flooded everything with radiation. Now the mass in number-three rocket is building and wildcatting itself. If it gets any higher, it'll explode."

"Why didn't your power-deck man dump the mass?" asked Strong.

"We didn't know it was wildcatting until after he had tried to repair it. And he didn't tighten the bolts enough to keep it from leaking radiation." The young skipper paused. "He lived long enough to warn us, though."

"What's the Geiger count on the radiation?" asked Strong.

"Up to twelve thirty-two—about ten minutes ago," answered James. "I pulled everybody out of the power deck and cut all energy circuits, including the energizing pumps. We didn't have any power so I had to use the combined juice of the three jet boats to send out the emergency signal that you picked up." He turned to face the little man with the glasses. "I had a choice of either saving about fifteen passengers on the jet boats, and leaving the others, or take a chance on saving everybody by using the power to send out a message."

"Ummmmh," said Strong to himself. He felt confidence in a young spaceman who would take a decision like that on himself. "What was that Geiger count again?" he asked.

"Must be better than fourteen hundred by now," answered James.

Strong made a quick decision.

"All right," he said, tight-lipped, "abandon ship! How many passengers?"

"Seventeen women and twenty-three men including the crew," replied James.

"Does that include yourself?" asked Strong.

"No," came the reply.

Strong felt better. Any man who would not count himself on a list to survive could be counted on in any emergency.

"We'll take four women at a time in each jet boat first," said Strong. "James, you and I will operate the jet boats and ferry the passengers to the *Polaris*. Tom, you and Roger and Astro get everybody aboard the ship ready to leave."

"Yes, sir," said Tom.

"We haven't much time. The reaction mass is building fast. Come on, James, we have to rip out the seats in the jet boats to get five people in them." Strong turned back into the jet-boat launching well.

"May I have the passenger lists, Captain?" asked Tom, turning to James. The young skipper handed him a clip board with the names of the passengers and crew and followed Strong.

"We will abandon ship in alphabetical order," announced Tom. "Miss Nancy Anderson?"

A young girl about sixteen stepped forward.

"Just stand there by the hatch, Miss," said Tom. He glanced at the next name. "Miss Elizabeth Anderson?" Another girl, looking very much like the first, stepped forward and stood beside her sister.

"Mrs. John Bailey?" called Tom.

A gray-haired woman of about sixty stepped forward.

"Pardon me, sir, but I would rather remain with my husband, and go later with him."

"No—no, Mary," pleaded an elderly man, holding his arm around her shoulder. "Go now. I'll be all right. Won't I, sir?" He looked at Tom anxiously.

"I can't be sure, sir," said Tom. He found it difficult to control his voice as he looked down at the old couple, who couldn't weigh more than two hundred pounds between them.

"I'm going to stay," said the woman firmly.

"As you wish, Madam," said Tom. He looked at the list again. "Mrs. Helen Carson?"

A woman about thirty-five, carrying a young boy about four years old, stepped out and took her place beside the two sisters.

In a moment, the first eight passengers were assembled into two groups, helped into space suits, with a special portable suit for the little boy, and loaded in the jet boats. The red light over the hatch glowed, then went out. The first load of passengers had left the *Lady Venus*.

"They're pretty jumpy," Roger whispered, nodding toward the remaining passengers.

"Yeah," answered Tom. "Say, where's Astro?"

"I don't know. Probably went to take a look at the jet boats to see if one could be repaired so we'd have a third ferry running."

"Good idea," said Tom. "See if you can't cheer these people up, Roger. Tell them stories or sing songs—or better yet, get them to sing. Try to make them forget they're sitting on an atom bomb!"

"I can't forget it myself," said Roger. "How can I make them forget it?"

"Try anything. I'll go see if I can't give Astro a hand!"

Roger turned to face the assembled passengers and smiled. All around him in the main passenger lounge, the frightened men and women sat huddled together in small groups, staring at him, terror in their eyes.

"Ladieeees and Gentlemen," began Roger. "You are now going to be entertained by the loudest, corniest and most miserable voice in the universe. I'm going to *sing*!"

He waited for a laugh, but there was only a slight stir as the passengers shifted nervously in their seats.

Shrugging his shoulders, Roger took a deep breath and began to sing. He only knew one song and he sang it with gusto.

> "From the rocket fields of the Academy
> To the far-flung stars of outer space,
> We're Space Cadets training to be . . ."

On the lower deck of the passenger ship, Tom smiled as he faintly heard his unit-mate's voice. He made his way to the jet-boat deck of the *Lady Venus* and opened the hatch.

"Hey, Astro," he called. There wasn't any answer.

He stepped inside and looked around the empty deck. Walking over to one of the jet boats, he saw evidence of Al James's attempts to send out emergency signal messages. He called again. "Hey, Astro—where are you?" Still no answer. He noticed that one of the jet boats was missing. There were three still on the deck, but an empty catapult for the fourth made Tom think that Astro might have repaired the fourth and taken it out in space for a test. The light over the escape hatch indicated that someone had gone out. It was odd, thought Tom, for Astro to go out alone. But then he shrugged, remembering how Astro could lose himself in his work and forget everything but the job at hand. He climbed back to the passenger deck.

When Tom opened the hatch to the main lounge, the sight that filled his eyes was so funny that, even in the face of danger, he had to laugh. Roger, with his hands clasped behind his back, was down on his knees trying to push a food pellet across the deck with his nose. The whole passenger lounge echoed with hysterical laughter.

Suddenly the laughter was stopped by the sound of the bell over the air-lock hatch. Strong and James had returned to ferry more passengers to the *Polaris*. Immediately the fun was forgotten and the passengers crowded around for the roll call.

"Where's Astro?" asked Strong, as he reappeared in the lounge.

"He's down on the jet-boat deck, sir, trying to fix another one," replied Tom. "I think he's out testing one now."

"Good," said Strong. "How're they taking it?" He indicated the passengers.

"Roger's been keeping them amused with games and songs, sir," said Tom proudly.

"They'll need it. I don't mind telling you, Corbett," said Strong, "it's a wonder to me this tub hasn't blown up already."

In less than a half hour, the forty passengers and crewmen of the *Lady Venus* were transferred in alphabetical order to the waiting *Polaris*. Roger kept up a continual line of patter and jokes and stories, making a fool of himself, but keeping the remaining passengers amused and their minds off the dangers of the rapidly building reaction mass.

"Just one passenger left," said Strong, "with myself and you three. I think we can squeeze five in that jet boat and get off here."

"That's for me," said Roger. "I'm the only man in the whole universe that's ever played to a packed house sitting on top of an atomic bomb!"

"All right, Barrymore," said Strong, "get aboard!"

"Say," asked Tom, "where's Astro?"

"I don't know," replied Roger. "I thought you went to find him half an hour ago!"

"I did," said Tom, "but when I went to the jet-boat deck, one was missing. So I figured he had fixed one and taken it out for a test."

"Then he's probably outside in space now!" said Strong. Suddenly the Solar Guard captain caught himself. "Wait a minute! How many jet boats were on the deck, Corbett?"

"Three, sir."

"Then Astro is still aboard the ship," said Strong. "He couldn't have taken a boat. James told me he couldn't repeat the message he sent out because he only had the power of *three* jet boats. One was damaged and left behind at Atom City!"

"By the rings of Saturn," said Roger, "a coupla million miles from home, sitting on an atomic bomb and that big Venusian hick decides to play hide-and-seek!"

"Never mind the cracks," said Strong. "We've got to find him!"

"Captain," said the little man with the round face and glasses who had first spoken to Strong when he came aboard, "just because my name happens to be Zewbriski, and I have to be the very last to get on a jet boat, I don't see why I have to wait any longer. I demand to be taken off this ship immediately! I refuse to risk my life waiting around for some foolish cadet!"

"That foolish cadet, Mr. Zewbriski," said Strong coldly, "is a human being like you and we don't budge until we find him!"

At that moment the bell began to ring, indicating that the outer hatch to the air lock was opening.

"By the craters of Luna," said Tom, "that must be Astro now!"

"But if it is," said Roger, "how did he get out there?"

From behind them, the hatch to the inner air lock opened and Al James stepped through.

"Captain Strong," he said excitedly, "you've got to come quickly. Some of the crewmen have broken into your arms locker and taken paralo-ray guns. They threaten to leave you here if you don't return to the ship within five minutes. They're afraid the *Venus* might blow up and damage the *Polaris* at this close range." The young skipper, his red-brown uniform torn and dirty, looked at the Solar Guard captain with wild-eyed desperation.

"They can't leave us here," whimpered Zewbriski. "We'll all be blown to bits!"

"Shut up!" barked Strong. He turned to Tom and Roger. "I can do one of two things," he said. "I can order you to return to the *Polaris* now, with James and myself, or you can volunteer to stay behind and search for Astro."

Without looking at Roger, Tom answered, "We'll stay, sir. And we won't have to search for him. I think I know where he is."

"Now that I think about it," replied Strong, "I guess there is only one place he could be."

"Yes, sir," said Tom, "down on the power deck trying to save this wagon! Come on, Roger! Let's get him!"

CHAPTER 15

"What's the reading on the Geiger counter now?" asked Tom.

Roger looked down at the face of the radioactive measuring device and answered, "She's been dropping for the last five minutes, Tom. Looks like the mass in number three is cooling off. Fourteen hundred and ten now."

"That's not fast enough," said Astro, straightening up from tightening a nut on the lead baffle. "She's still plenty hot. That mass should have been dumped out of the rocket exhaust right away. Now the whole tube control box is so hot with radiation, it'd burn you to a crisp if you opened the hatch."

"Good thing you brought along those tools from the *Polaris*," said Tom.

"Yeah, greaseball," said Roger, "you used your head for once. Now let's see you use it again and pile out of this hunk of junk!"

"Fifteen hundred on the counter is the danger mark, Roger, and as long as we keep it under that, I'm going to try and save this wagon!" replied Astro.

"Why? To get yourself a Solar Medal?" asked Roger sarcastically.

"What do you think made this tub act up like this, Astro?" asked Tom, ignoring Roger's remark.

"Using special reactant feed, Tom," replied Astro. "This is a converted chemical burner—with an old-type cooling pump. It's touchy stuff."

"Well, couldn't we drive boron rods into the mass and slow down the reaction?" asked Tom.

"No, Tom," answered Astro, "the control for the rods are inside the tube control box. We can't reach it."

There was a sudden loud ticking from the Geiger counter.

"Astro!" cried Roger. "The mass is building!"

"Here, lemme see!" shouted Astro. He took the instrument in his big hand and watched the clocklike face intently.

"... fourteen hundred thirty—fourteen hundred fifty—fourteen hundred seventy—" He faced his unit-mates. "Well, that does it. The mass is maintaining a steady reaction without the energizing pumps. It's sustaining itself!"

"But how is that possible?" asked Tom.

"It's one of those freaks, Tom. It's been known to happen before. The fuel is just hot enough to sustain a steady reaction because of its high intensity. Once that baffle worked loose, the mass started wildcatting itself."

"And if it doesn't stop?" asked Roger tensely.

"It'll reach a point where the reaction comes so fast it'll explode!"

"Let's pile out of here!" said Roger.

The three boys made a dash for their space suits and the jet boat. Inside the air lock, they adjusted their oxygen valves and waited for pressure to equalize so they could blast off.

"Blast it," said Astro, "there must be some way to get to that rocket tube and dump that stuff!"

"Impossible, Astro," said Roger. "The release controls are in the control box, and with all that radiation loose, you wouldn't last half a minute!"

Tom walked over to the valve that would open the outside hatch.

"Wonder how Captain Strong is making out with those tough babies on the *Polaris*?" asked Tom.

"I don't know," replied Roger, "but anything would be better than sitting around waiting for this thing to blow up!"

"Ah—stop griping," said Astro, "or I'll shove you up a rocket tube and blast you from here all the way back to Atom City!"

"Hey, wait a minute!" shouted Tom. "Astro, remember the time we were on the ground crew as extra duty and we had to overhaul the *Polaris*?"

"Yeah, why?"

"There was one place you couldn't go. You were too big, so I went in, remember?"

"Yeah, the space between the rocket tubes and the hull of the ship. It was when we were putting in the new tube. So what?"

"So this!" said Tom. "When they converted this tub, they had standard exhausts, so it must have the same layout as the *Polaris*. Suppose I climb in the main exhaust, between the tube and the outer hull, and cut away the cleats that hold the tube to the ship?"

"Why, then everything would come out in one piece!" Astro's face lit up. "Reactant mass, tube, control box—the works!"

"Say, what are you two guys talking about?" asked Roger.

"Saving a ship, Roger," said Tom. "Dumping the whole assembly of the number-three rocket!"

"Ah—you're space happy!"

"Maybe," said Tom, "but I think it's worth trying. How about it, Astro?"

"O.K. by me, Tom," replied Astro.

"Good. You get the cutting torches rigged, Astro. Roger, you give him a hand and keep your eye on the counter. Then feed the torches to me when I get inside the tube. I'm going outside to get rid of a bad rocket and save a five-million-credit spaceship!"

Before Astro or Roger could protest, Tom opened the hatch and began to climb out on the steel hull toward the rocket tubes, main exhaust.

His magnetic-soled shoes gripping the smooth steel hull, the cadet made his way aft to the stern of the ship and began the climb down around the huge firing tubes and into the tubes themselves.

"Hey, Astro," he yelled into the spacephone, "I'm inside the tubes. How about those torches?" The cadets had adjusted the wave length so that all could hear what was said.

"Take it easy, spaceboy," said Roger, "I'm leaving the hatch now. You and your fatheaded friend from Venus are so hopped up for getting a Solar Medal—"

"Knock it off, Manning!" said Astro from inside the ship. "And for your information, I don't want a medal. I don't want anything except for you to stop griping!"

Roger reached the end of the ship and began to climb down inside the tube where Tom was waiting for him.

"O.K., spaceboy," said Roger, "here're your cutting torches." He started moving back. "I'll see you around. I don't mind being a little hero for saving people and all that stuff. But not for any ship. And the odds against a big hero staying alive are too big!"

"Roger, wait," shouted Tom. "I'll need . . ." And then the curly-headed cadet clamped his teeth together and turned back to the task at hand.

He made adjustments on the nozzle of the cutting torch, and then, focusing his chest light, called to Astro.

"O.K., Astro," he said, "shoot me the juice!"

"Coming up, Tom!" answered Astro. "And wait till I get my hands on that Manning! I'm going to smear that yellow space crawler from one corner of the universe to another!"

"Never mind the talk," snarled Roger, who at the moment was re-entering the tube. "Just get that juice down to this torch and make it fast!"

Tom turned to see Roger crawling back into the tube and adjusting a cutting torch.

"Glad to have you aboard, Roger," said Tom with a smile that Roger could not see in the darkness of the tube. The two boys went to work.

Suddenly the torches came to life. And immediately Tom and Roger began to cut away at the cleats that held the tube lining to the skin of the ship. Steadily, the cadets worked their way up toward the center of the ship, cutting anything that looked as though it might hold the giant tube to the ship.

"Boy," said Tom, "it's getting hot in here!"

From inside the ship, Astro's reassuring voice came back in answer. "You're getting close to the reactant-mass chamber. The last cleat is up by one of the exhaust gratings. Think you can last it?"

"Well, if he can't," snarled Roger, "he's sure to get that medal anyway!" He inched up a little. "Move over, Corbett, I'm skinnier than you are, and I can reach that cleat easier than you can."

Roger slipped past Tom and inched his way toward the last cleat. He pulled his torch up alongside and pulled the trigger. The flame shot out and began eating the steel. In a moment the last cleat was cut and the two boys started their long haul down the tube to the outside of the ship.

As they walked across the steel surface, back to the air lock, Tom stuck out his hand.

"I'm glad you came back, Roger."

"Save it for the boys that fall for that stuff, Corbett," said Roger sarcastically. "I came back because I didn't want you and that Venusian hick to think you're the only ones with guts around here!"

"No one has ever accused you of not having guts, Roger."

"Ah—go blast your jets," snarled Roger.

They went directly to the power deck where Astro was waiting for them, the Geiger counter in his hand.

"All set to get rid of the rotten apple?" he asked with a smile.

"All set, Astro," said Tom. "What's the count?"

"She seems to have steadied around fourteen hundred ninety—and believe me, the ten points to the official danger mark of fifteen hundred is so small that we could find out where the angels live any moment now!"

"Then what're we waiting for," said Tom. "Let's dump that thing!"

"How?" snarled Roger.

Tom and Astro looked at him bewilderedly. "What do you mean 'how'?" asked Astro.

"I mean how are you going to get the tube out of the ship?"

"Why," started Tom, "there's nothing holding that tube assembly to the ship now. We cut all the cleats, remember? We can jettison the whole unit!"

"It seems to me," drawled Roger lazily, "that the two great heroes in their mad rush for the Solar Medal have forgotten an unwritten law of space. There's no gravity out here—no natural force to pull or push the tube. The only way it could be moved is by the power of thrust, either forward or backward!"

"O.K. Then let's push it out, just that way," said Astro.

"How?" asked Roger cynically.

"Simple, Roger," said Tom, "Newton's Laws of motion. Everything in motion tends to keep going at the same speed unless influenced by an outside force. So if we blasted our nose rockets and started going backward, everything on the ship would go backward too, then if we reversed—"

Astro cut in, "Yeah—if we blasted the stern rockets, the ship would go forward, but the tube, being loose, would keep going the other way!"

"There's only one thing wrong," said Roger. "That mass is so hot now, if any booster energy hit it, it would be like a trigger on a bomb. It'd blow us from here to the next galaxy!"

"I'm willing to try it," said Tom. "How about you, Astro?"

"I've gone this far, and I'm not quitting now."

They turned to face Roger.

"Well, how about it, Roger?" asked Tom. "No one will think you're yellow if you take the jet boat and leave now."

"Ah—talk again!" grumbled Roger. "We always have to talk. Let's be original for a change and just do our jobs!"

"All right," said Tom. "Take an emergency light and signal Captain Strong. Tell him what we're going to do. Warn him to stay away—about two hundred miles off. He'll know if we're successful or not within a half hour!"

"Yeah," said Roger, "then we'll send him one big flash to mean we failed! *Bon voyage!*"

Fifteen minutes later, as the *Lady Venus* drifted in her silent but deadly orbit, Tom, Roger and Astro still worked feverishly as the Geiger counter ticked off the increasing radioactivity of the wildcatting reaction mass in number-three rocket tube.

"Reading on the counter still's going up, Astro," warned Roger. "Fifteen-O-five."

"Hurry it up, Astro," urged Tom.

"Hand me that wrench, Tom," ordered Astro. The big cadet, stripped to the waist, his thick arms and chest splattered with grease and sweat, fitted the wrench to the nut and applied pressure. Tom and Roger watched the muscles ripple along his back, as the big Venusian pitted all of his great strength against the metal.

"Give it all you've got," said Tom. "If we do manage to jettison that tube, we've got to keep this part of the power deck airtight!"

Astro pulled harder. The veins standing out on his neck. At last, easing off, he stood up and looked down at the nut.

"That's as tight as I can get it," he said, breathing heavily.

"Or anyone else," said Tom.

"All the valve connections broken?" asked Astro.

"Yep," replied Roger. "We're sealed tight."

"That's it, then," said Tom. "Let's get to the control deck and start blasting!"

Astro turned to the power-deck control board and checked the gauges for the last time. From above his head, he heard Tom's voice over the intercom.

"All your relays to the power deck working, Astro?"

"Ready, Tom," answered Astro.

"Then stand by," said Tom on the control deck. He had made a hasty check of the controls and found them to be similar enough to those on the *Polaris* so that he could handle the ship. He flipped the switch to the radar deck and spoke into the intercom.

"Do we have a clear trajectory fore and aft, Roger?"

"All clear," replied Roger. "I sent Captain Strong the message."

"What'd he say?"

"The rebellion wasn't anything more than a bunch of badly scared old men. Al James just got hysterical, that's all."

A low muted roar pulsed through the ship

"What did he have to say about this operation?"

"I can't repeat it for your young ears," said Roger.

"So bad, huh?"

"Yeah, but not because we're trying to save the ship."

"Then why?" asked Tom.

"He's afraid of losing a good unit!"

Tom smiled and turned to the control board. "Energize the cooling pumps!" he bawled to Astro over the intercom.

The slow whine of the pumps began to build to a shrieking pitch.

"Pumps in operation, Tom," said Astro.

"Cut in nose braking rockets," ordered Tom.

A low muted roar pulsed through the ship.

"Rockets on—we're moving backward, Tom," reported Astro.

And then suddenly Astro let out a roar. "Tom, the Geiger counter is going wild!"

"Never mind that now," answered Tom. "Sound off, Roger!" he yelled.

"Ship moving astern—one thousand feet a second—two thousand—four thousand—"

"I'm going to let her build to ten, Roger," yelled Tom. "We've only got one chance and we might as well make it a good one!"

"Six thousand!" yelled Roger. "Seven thousand!"

"Astro," bellowed Tom, "stand by to fire stern rockets!"

"Ready, Tom," was Astro's reply.

"Eight thousand," warned Roger. "Spaceman's luck, fellas!"

The silver ship moved through space away from the *Polaris*.

"Nine thousand," reported Roger. "And, Astro, I really love ya!"

"Cut nose braking rockets!" ordered Tom.

There was a sudden hush that seemed to be as loud as the noise of the rockets. The huge passenger ship, *Lady Venus*, was traveling through space as silent as a ghost.

"Nine thousand five hundred feet a second," yelled Roger.

"Stand by, Astro, Roger! Hang on tight, and spaceman's luck!"

"Ten thousand feet a second!" Roger's voice was a hoarse scream.

"*Fire stern rockets!*" bawled Tom.

CHAPTER 16

Under the tremendous drive of the stern rockets, the silver ship suddenly hurtled forward as if shot out of a cannon. The dangerous tube slid out of the stern of the ship and was quickly left behind as the *Lady Venus* sped in the opposite direction.

"That's it," yelled Tom, "hold full space speed! We dumped the tube, but we're still close enough for it to blow us from here to Pluto!"

"I tracked it on the radar, Tom," yelled Roger. "I think we're far enough away to miss—"

At that moment a tremendous flash of light filled the radar scanner as the mass exploded miles to the rear of the *Lady Venus*.

"There it goes!" shouted Roger.

"Great jumping Jupiter," yelled Tom, "and we're still in one piece! We did it!"

From the power deck, Astro's bull-like roar could be heard through the whole ship.

"Gimme an open circuit, Tom," said Astro. "I want to operate the air blowers down here and try to get rid of some of that radiation. I have to get into the control chamber and see what's going on."

Tom flipped a switch on the board and set the ship on automatic flight. Then, turning to the teleceiver, he switched the set on.

"*Lady Venus* to *Polaris*—" said Tom, "come in, *Polaris*—come in!"

". . . Strong here on the *Polaris*!" the officer's voice crackled over the speaker. "By the rings of Saturn, I should log you three space-brained idiots for everything in the book!" Strong's face gradually focused on the teleceiver screen and he stared at Tom coldly. "That was the most foolish bit of heroics I've ever seen and if I had my way I'd—I'll—well—" The captain's glare melted into a smile. "I'll spend the rest of my life being known as the skipper of the three heroes! Well done, Corbett, it was foolish and dangerous, but well done!"

Tom, his face changing visibly with each change in Strong's attitude, finally broke out into a grin.

"Thank you, sir," said Tom, "but Astro and Roger did as much as I did."

"I'm sure they did," replied Strong. "Tell them I think it was one of the—the—" he thought a moment and then added, "darndest, most foolish things—most—"

"Yes, sir," said Tom, trying hard to control his face. He knew the moment for disciplining had passed, and that Captain Strong was just overwhelmed with concern for their safety.

"Stand by the air locks, Corbett, we're coming aboard again. We're pretty cramped for space here on the *Polaris*."

Just then Astro yelled up from the power deck.

"Hey, Tom!" he called. "If Captain Strong is thinking about putting those passengers back aboard, I think you'd better tell him about the radiation. I haven't been able to flush it all out yet. And since we only have three lead-lined suits . . ." He left the statement unfinished.

"I get you, Astro," replied Tom. He turned back to the teleceiver and faced Strong. "Astro says the ship is still hot from radiation, sir. And that he hasn't been able to flush it out with the blowers."

"Ummmmh," mused Strong thoughtfully. "Well, in that case, stand by, Corbett. I'll get in touch with Commander Walters right away."

"Very well, sir," replied Tom. He turned from the teleceiver and climbed up to the radar deck.

"Well, hot-shot," said Roger, "looks like you've made yourself a hero this trip."

"What do you mean by that, Roger?"

"First, you run off with top honors on the space maneuvers, and now you save the ship and have Strong eating out of your hand!"

"That's not very funny, Roger," said Tom.

"I think it is," drawled Roger.

Tom studied the blond cadet for a moment.

"What's eating you, Roger? Since the day you came into the Academy, you've acted like you hated every minute of it. And yet, on the other hand, I've seen you act like it was the most important thing in your life. Why?"

"I told you once, Corbett," said Roger with the sneering air which Tom knew he used when he was on the defensive, "that I had my own special reasons for being here. I'm *not* a hero, Corbett! Never was and never will be. You're strictly the hero type. Tried and true, a thousand just like you all through the Academy and the Solar Guard. Strong is a hero type!"

"Then what about Al James?" asked Tom. "What about that time in Atom City when you defended the Academy?"

"Uh-uh," grunted Roger, "I wasn't defending the Academy. I was just avoiding a fight." He paused and eyed Tom between half-closed lids. "You'll never do anything I can't, or won't do, just as well, Tom. The difference between us is simple. I'm in the Academy for a reason, a special reason. You're here, like most of the other cadets, because you believe in it. That's the difference between you, me and Astro. You believe in it. I don't—I don't believe in anything but Roger Manning!"

Tom faced him squarely. "I'm not going to buy that, Roger! I don't think that's true. And the reasons I don't believe it are many. You have a chip on your shoulder, yes. But I don't think you're selfish or that you only believe in Manning. If you did, you wouldn't be here on the *Lady Venus*. You had your chance to escape back in the rocket tube, but you *came back*, Roger, and you made a liar out of yourself!"

"Hey, you guys!" yelled Astro, coming up behind them. "I thought we left that stuff back at the Academy?"

Tom turned to face the power-deck cadet. "What's cooking below, Astro? Were you able to get rid of the radiation?"

"Naw!" replied the cadet from Venus. "Too hot! Couldn't even open the hatch. It'll take a special job with the big equipment at the space shipyards. We need their big blowers and antiradiation flushers to clean this baby up."

"Then I'd better tell Captain Strong right away. He's going to get in touch with Commander Walters at the Academy for orders."

"Yeah, you're right," said Astro. "There isn't a chance of getting those people back aboard here now. Once we opened up that outer control deck to dump that tube, the whole joint started buzzing with radioactive electrons."

Tom turned to the ladder leading to the control deck and disappeared through the hatch, leaving Astro and Roger alone.

"What was that little bit of space gas about, Roger?"

"Ah—nothing," replied Roger. "Just a little argument on who was the biggest hero." Roger smiled and waved a hand in a friendly gesture. "Tom won, two to one!"

"He sure handled that control deck like he had been born here, all right," said Astro. "Well, I've got to take a look at those motors. We'll be doing something soon, and whatever it is, we'll need those power boxes to get us where we want to go."

"Yeah," said Roger, "and I've got to get a course and a position." He turned to the chart screen and began plotting rapidly. Down on the control deck, Strong was listening to Tom.

" . . . and Astro said we'd need the special equipment at the space shipyards to clean out the radiation, sir. If we took passengers aboard and it suddenly shot up—well, we only have the three lead-lined suits to protect us."

"Very well, Corbett," replied Strong. "I've just received orders from Commander Walters to proceed to Mars with both ships. I'll blast off now and you three follow along on the *Lady Venus*. Any questions?"

"I don't have any, sir," Tom said, "but I'll check with Roger and Astro to see if they have any."

Tom turned to the intercom and informed the radar and power-deck cadets of their orders, and asked if there were any questions. Both replied that everything on the ship was ready to blast off immediately. Tom turned back to the teleceiver.

"No questions, sir," reported Tom. "We're all set to blast off."

"Very well, Corbett," said Strong. "I'm going to make as much speed as possible to get these people on Mars. The crew of the *Lady Venus* will take over the radar and power decks."

"O.K., sir, and spaceman's luck!" said Tom. "We'll see you on Mars!"

Tom stood beside the crystal port on the control deck and watched the rocket cruiser *Polaris'* stern glow red from her jets, and then quickly disappear into the vastness of space, visible only as a white blip on the radar scanner.

"Get me a course to Mars, Roger," said Tom. "Astro, stand by to blast off with as much speed as you can safely get out of this old wagon, and stand by for Mars!"

The two cadets quickly reported their departments ready, and following the course Roger plotted, Astro soon had the *Lady Venus* blasting through space, heading for Mars!

Mars, fourth planet in order from the Sun, loomed like a giant red gem against a perfect backdrop of deep-black space. The *Lady Venus*, rocketing through the inky blackness, a dull red glow from her three remaining rockets, blasted steadily ahead to the planet that was crisscrossed with wide spacious canals.

"Last time I was on Mars," said Astro to Tom and Roger over a cup of tea, "was about two years ago. I was bucking rockets on an old tub called the *Space Plunger*. It was on a shuttle run from the Martian south pole to Venusport, hauling vegetables. What a life! Burning up on Venus and then freezing half to death at the south pole on Mars." Astro shook his head as the vivid memory took him back for a moment.

"From what I hear," said Tom, "there isn't much to see but the few cities, the mountains, the deserts and the canals."

"Yeah," commented Roger, "big deal! Rocket into the wild depths of space and see the greatest hunk of wasteland in the universe!"

The three boys were silent, listening to the steady hum of the rockets, driving them forward toward Mars. For four days they had traveled on the *Lady Venus*, enjoying the many luxuries found on the passenger ship. Now, with their destination only a few hours away, they were having a light snack before making a touchdown on Mars.

"You know," said Tom quietly, "I've been thinking. As far back as the twentieth century, Earthmen have wanted to get to Mars. And finally they did. And what have they found? Nothing but a planet full of dry sand, a few canals and dwarf mountains."

"That's exactly what I've been saying!" said Roger. "The only man who ever got anything out of all this was the first man to make it to Mars and return. He got the name, the glory, and a paragraph in a history book! And after that, nothing!" He got up and climbed the ladder to the radar deck, leaving Astro and Tom alone.

Suddenly the ship lurched to one side.

"What's that?" cried Tom.

A bell began to ring. Then another—and then three more. Finally the entire ship was vibrating with the clanging of emergency bells.

Astro made a diving leap for the ladder leading down to the power deck, with Tom lunging for the control board.

Quickly Tom glanced about the huge board with its many different gauges and dials, searching for the one that would indicate the trouble. His eye spotted a huge gauge. A small light beside it flashed off and on. "By the moons of Jupiter, we've run out of reactant fuel!"

"Tom!—Tom!" shouted Astro from the power deck. "We're smack out of reactant feed!"

"Isn't there any left at all?" asked Tom. "Not even enough to get us into Marsopolis?"

"We haven't enough left to keep the generator going!" said Astro. "Everything, including the lights and the televeiver, will go any minute!"

"Then we can't change course!"

"Right," drawled Roger. "And if we can't change course, the one we're on now will take us straight into Mars's gravity and we crash!"

"Send out an emergency call right away, Roger," said Tom.

"Can't, spaceboy," replied Roger in his lazy drawl. "Not enough juice to call for help. Or haven't you noticed you're standing in the dark?"

"But how—how could this happen?" asked Tom, puzzled. "We were only going at half speed and using just three rockets!"

"When we got rid of that hot tube back in space," explained Astro grimly, "we dumped the main reactant mass. There isn't a thing we can do!"

"We've got one choice," said Tom hollowly. "We can either pile out now, in space suits and use the jet boat, and hope for someone to pick us up before the oxygen gives out, or we can ride this space wagon right on in. Make up your minds quick, we're already inside Mars's gravity pull!"

There was a pause, then Astro's voice filled the control deck. "I'll ride this baby right to the bottom. If I'm going to splash in, I'll take it on solid ground, even if it is Mars and not Venus. I don't want to wash out in space!"

"That goes for me, too," said Roger.

"O.K.," said Tom. "Here we go. Just keep your fingers crossed that we hit the desert instead of the mountains, or we'll be smeared across those rocks like applesauce. Spaceman's luck, fellas!"

"Spaceman's luck, both of you," said Astro.

"Just plain ordinary luck," commented Roger, "and plenty of it!"

The three boys quickly strapped themselves into acceleration seats, with Tom hooking up an emergency relay switch that he could hold in his hand. He hoped he would remain conscious long enough to throw the switch and start the water sprinkler in case the ship caught fire.

The *Lady Venus* flashed into the thin atmosphere from the void of space and the three cadets imagined that they could hear the shriek of the ship as it cut through the thin air. Tom figured his speed rapidly, and counting on the thinness of the atmosphere, he estimated that it would take eleven seconds for the ship to crash. He began to count.

" . . . One—two—three—four—five—" he thought briefly of his family and how nice they had been to him " . . . six—seven—eight—nine—ten—"

The ship crashed.

CHAPTER 17

"Astro! Roger!" yelled Tom. He opened his eyes and then felt the weight on his chest. A section of the control board had fallen across him pinning his left arm to his side. He reached for the railing around the acceleration chair with his right and discovered he still held the switch for the water sprinkler. He started to flip it on, then sniffed the air, and smelling no trace of smoke, dropped the switch. He unstrapped himself from the acceleration chair with his right hand and then slowly, with great effort, pushed the section of the control board off him. He stood up rubbing his left arm.

"Astro? Roger?!" he called again, and scrambled over the broken equipment that was strewn over the deck. He stumbled over more rubble that was once a precision instrument panel and climbed the ladder leading to the radar deck.

"Roger!" he yelled. "Roger, are you all right?" He pushed several shattered instruments out of the way and looked around the shambles that once had been a room. He didn't see Roger.

He began to scramble through the litter on the deck, kicking aside instruments that were nearly priceless, so delicately were they made. Suddenly a wave of cold fear gripped him and he began tearing through the rubble desperately. From beneath a heavy tube casing, he could see the outstretched arm of Roger.

He squatted down, bending his legs and keeping his back straight. Then gripping the heavy casing on one side, he tried to stand up. It was too much for him. He lifted it three inches and then had to let go.

"Tom! Roger!" Tom heard the bull-like roar of Astro below him and stumbled over to the head of the ladder.

"Up here, Astro," he yelled, "on the radar deck. Roger's pinned under the radar scanner casing!"

Tom turned back to the casing, and looking around the littered deck desperately, grabbed an eight-foot length of steel pipe that had been snapped off like a twig by the force of the crash.

Barely able to lift it, he shoved it with all his strength to get the end of the pipe beneath the casing.

"Here, let me get at that thing," growled Astro from behind. Tom stepped back, half falling out of the Venusian's way, and watched as Astro got down on his hands and knees, putting his shoulder against the case. He lifted it about three inches, then slowly, still balancing the weight on his shoulder, shifted his position, braced it with his hands and began to straighten up. The casing came up from the floor as the huge cadet strained against it.

"All—right—Tom—" he gasped, "see if you can get a hold on Roger and pull him out!"

Tom scrambled back and grabbed Roger's uniform. He pulled, and slowly the cadet's form slid from beneath the casing.

"All right, Astro," said Tom, "I've got 'im."

Astro began to lower the casing in the same manner in which he had lifted it. He eased it back down to the floor on his knees and dropped it the last few inches. He sat on the floor beside it and hung his head between his knees.

"Are you all right, Astro?" asked Tom.

"Never mind me," panted Astro between deep gasps for breath, "just see if hot-shot is O.K."

Tom quickly ran his hands up and down Roger's arms and legs, his chest, collarbone and at last, with gently probing fingers, his head.

"No broken bones," he said, still looking at Roger, "but I don't know about internal injuries."

"He wasn't pinned under that thing," said Astro at last. "It was resting on a beam. No weight was on him."

"Uh—huh—ahhh—uhhhh," moaned Roger.

"Roger," said Tom gently, "Roger, are you all right?"

"Uh—huh?—Ohhhh! My head!"

"Take it easy, hot-shot," said Astro, "that head of yours is O.K. Nothing—but *nothing* could hurt it!"

"Ooohhhh!" groaned Roger, sitting up. "I don't know which is worse, feeling the way I do, or waking up and listening to you again!"

Tom sat back with a smile. Roger's remark clinched it. No one was hurt.

"Well," said Astro at last, "where do we go from here?"

"First thing I suggest we do is take a survey and see what's left," said Tom.

"I came up from the power deck," said Astro, "all the way through the ship. You see this radar deck?" He made a sweeping gesture around the room that looked like a junk heap. "Well, it's in good shape, compared to the rest of the ship. The power deck has the rocket motors where the master panel should be and the panel is ready to go into what's left of the reactant chamber. The jet boat is nothing but a worthless piece of junk!"

The three boys considered the fate of the jet boat soberly. Finally Astro broke the silence with a question. "Where do you think we are?"

"Somewhere in the New Sahara desert," answered Tom. "I had the chart projector on just before we splashed in, but I can't tell you any more than that."

"Well, at least we have plenty of water," sighed Roger.

"You *had* plenty of water. The tanks were smashed when we came in. Not even a puddle left in a corner."

"Of course it might rain," said Roger.

Tom gave a short laugh. "The last time it rained in this place dinosaurs were roaming around on Earth!"

"How about food?" asked Roger.

"Plenty of that," answered Astro. "This is a passenger ship, remember! They have everything you could ask for, including smoked Venusian fatfish!"

"Then let's get out of here and take a look," said Tom.

The three bruised but otherwise healthy cadets climbed slowly down to the control deck and headed for the galley, where Tom found six plastic containers of Martian water.

"Spaceman, this is the biggest hunk of luck we've had in the last two hours," said Roger, taking one of the containers.

"Why two hours, Roger?" asked Astro, puzzled.

"Two hours ago we were still in space expecting to splash in," said Tom. He opened one of the containers and offered it to Astro. "Take it easy, Astro," said Tom. "Unless we find something else to drink, this might have to last a long time."

"Yeah," said Roger, "a *long* time. I've been thinking about our chances of getting out of this mess."

"Well," asked Astro, "what has the great Manning brain figured out?"

"There's no chance at all," said Roger slowly. "You're wrong, Corbett, about this being midday. It's early morning!" He pointed to a chronometer on the bulkhead behind Astro. "It's still running. I made a mental note before we splashed in, it was eight-O-seven. That clock says nine-O-three. It doesn't begin to get hot here until three o'clock in the afternoon."

"I think you're wrong two ways," said Tom. "In the first place, Captain Strong probably has a unit out looking for us right now. And in the second place, as long as we stay with the ship, we've got shade. That sun is only bad because the atmosphere is thinner here on Mars, and easier to burn through. But if we stay out of the sun, we're O.K. Just sit back and wait for Strong!"

Roger shrugged his shoulders.

"Well," commented Astro with a grin, "I'm not going to sit around waiting for Strong without eating!" He tore open a plastic package of roast-beef sandwiches and began eating. Tom measured out three small cups of Martian water.

"After we eat," suggested Roger, "I think we ought to take a look around outside and try to set up an identification signal."

"That's a good idea," said Tom, "but don't you think the ship itself is big enough for that?"

"Yeah," answered Roger, "I guess you're right."

"Boy!" said Astro. "We sure are lucky to still be able to argue."

"That's about all you can call it. Luck! Spaceman's luck!" said Tom. "The only reason I can figure why we didn't wind up as permanent part of the scenery around here is because of the course we were on."

"How do you figure that?" asked Astro.

"Luckily—and I *mean* luckily, we were on a course that took us smack onto the surface of Mars. And our speed was great enough to resist the gravity pull of the planet, keeping us horizontal with the surface of the desert. We skidded in like a kid does on a sled, instead of coming in on our nose!"

"Well, blast my jets!" said Astro softly.

"In that case," said Roger, "we must have left a pretty long skid mark in back of us!"

"That should be easy to see when the jet scouts come looking for us," commented Astro.

"I wonder if we could rig up some sort of emergency signal so we could send out a relative position?"

"How are you going to get the position?" asked Astro.

"I can give you some sort of position as soon as I get outside and take a sight on the sun," replied Roger.

"Can you do it without your astrogation prism?" asked Astro.

"Navigation, not astrogation, Astro," said Roger. "Like the ancient sailors used on the oceans back on Earth hundreds of years ago. Only thing is, I'll have to work up the logarithms by hand, instead of using the computer. Might be a little rough, but it'll be close enough for what we want."

The three cadets finished the remaining sandwiches and then picked their way back through the ship to the control deck. There, they rummaged through the pile of broken and shattered instruments.

"If we could find just one tube that hasn't been damaged, I think I might be able to rig up some sort of one-lung communications set," said Roger. "It might have enough range to get a message to the nearest atmosphere booster station."

"Nothing but a pile of junk here, Roger," said Tom. "We might find something on the radar deck."

The three members of the *Polaris* unit climbed over the rubble and made their way to the radar deck, and started their search for an undamaged tube. After forty-five minutes of searching, Roger stood up in disgust.

"Nothing!" he said sourly.

"That kills any hope of getting a message out," said Tom.

"By the craters of Luna," said Astro, wiping his forehead. "I didn't notice it before, but it's getting hotter here than on the power deck on a trip to Mercury!"

"Do we have any flares?" asked Roger.

"Naw. Al James used them all," answered Tom.

"That does it," said Roger. "In another couple of hours, when and if anyone shows up, all they'll find is three space cadets fried on the half shell of a spaceship!"

"Listen, Roger," said Tom, "as soon as we fail to check in, the whole Mars Solar Guard fleet will be out looking for us. Our last report will show them we were heading in this direction. It won't take Captain Strong long to figure out that we might have run out of fuel, and, with that skid mark in the sand trailing back for twenty miles, all we have to do is stick with the ship and wait for them to show up!"

"What's that?" asked Astro sharply.

From a distance, the three cadets could hear a low moaning and wailing. They rushed to the crystal port and looked out on the endless miles of brown sand, stretching as far as the horizon and meeting the cloudless blue sky. Shimmering in the heat, the New Sahara desert of Mars was just beginning to warm up for the day under the bleaching sun. The thin atmosphere offered little protection against the blazing heat rays.

"Nothing but sand," said Tom. "Maybe something is still hot on the power deck." He looked at Astro.

"I checked it before I came topside," said Astro. "I've heard that noise before. It can only mean one thing."

"What's that?" asked Roger.

Astro turned quickly and walked to the opposite side of the littered control deck. He pushed a pile of junk out of the way for a clear view of the outside.

"There's your answer," said Astro, pointing at the port.

"By the rings of Saturn, look at that!" cried Tom.

"Yeah," said Roger, "black as the fingernails of a Titan miner!"

"That's a sandstorm," Astro said finally. "It blows as long as a week and can pile up sand for two hundred feet. Sometimes the velocity reaches as much as a hundred and sixty miles an hour. Once, in the south, we got caught in one, and it was so bad we had to blast off. And it took all the power we had to do it!"

The three cadets stood transfixed as they gazed through the crystal port at the oncoming storm. The tremendous black cloud rolled toward the spaceship in huge folds that billowed upward and back in three-thousand-foot waves. The roar and wail of the wind grew louder, rising in pitch until it was a shrill scream.

"We'd better get down to the power deck," said Tom, "and take some oxygen bottles along with us, just in case. Astro, bring the rest of the Martian water and you grab several of those containers of food, Roger. We might be holed in for a long time."

"Why go down to the power deck?" asked Roger.

"There's a huge hole in the upper part of the ship's hull. That sand will come in here by the ton and there's nothing to stop it," Tom answered Roger, but kept his eyes on the churning black cloud. Already, the first gusts of wind were lashing at the stricken *Lady Venus*.

CHAPTER 18

"You think it'll last much longer?" asked Astro.

"I don't know, old fellow," replied Tom.

"You know, sometimes you can hear the wind even through the skin of the ship," commented Roger.

For two days the cadets of the *Polaris* unit had been held prisoner in the power deck while the violence of the New Sahara sandstorm raged around them outside the ship. For a thousand square miles the desert was a black cloud of churning sand, sweeping across the surface of Mars like a giant shroud.

After many attempts to repair a small generator, Astro finally succeeded, only to discover that he had no means of running the unit. His plan was to relieve the rapidly weakening emergency batteries with a more steady source of power.

While Astro occupied himself repairing the generator, Tom and Roger had slept, but after the first day, when sleep would no longer come, they resorted to playing checkers with washers and nuts on a board scratched on the deck.

"Think it's going to let up soon?" asked Roger.

"They've been known to last for a week or more," said Astro.

"Wonder if Strong has discovered we're missing?" mused Roger.

"Sure he has," replied Tom. "He's a real spaceman. Can smell out trouble like a telemetered alarm system."

Astro got up and stretched. "I'll bet we're out of this five hours after the sand settles down."

The big Venusian walked to the side of the power deck and pressed his ear against the hull, listening for the sound of the wind.

After a few seconds he turned back. "I can't hear a thing, fellas. I have a feeling it's about played itself out."

"Of course," reasoned Tom, "we have no real way of knowing when it's stopped and when it hasn't."

"Want to open the hatch and take a look?" asked Astro.

Tom looked questioningly at Roger, who nodded his head in agreement.

Tom walked over to the hatch and began undogging the heavy door. As the last of the heavy metal bars were raised, sand began to trickle inside around the edges. Astro bent down and sifted a handful through his fingers. "It's so fine, it's like powder," he said as it fell to the deck in a fine cloud.

"Come on," said Tom, "give me a hand with this hatch. It's probably jammed up against sand on the other side."

Tom, Roger and Astro braced their shoulders against the door, but when they tried to push, they lost their footing and slipped down. Astro dragged over a section of lead baffle, jammed it between the rocket motors and placed his feet up against it. Tom and Roger got on either side of him and pressed their shoulders against the door.

"All right," said Tom. "When I give the word, let's all push together. Ready?"

"All set," said Astro.

"Let's go," said Roger.

"O.K.—then—one—two—three—*push!*"

Together, the three cadets strained against the heavy steel hatch. The muscles in Astro's legs bulged into knots as he applied his great weight and strength against the door. Roger, his face twisted into a grimace from the effort, finally slumped to the floor, gasping for breath.

"Roger," asked Tom quickly, "are you all right?"

Roger nodded his head but stayed where he was, breathing deeply. Finally recovering his strength, he rose and stood up against the hatch with his two unit-mates.

"You and Roger just give a steady pressure, Tom," said Astro. "Don't try to push it all at once. Slow and steady does it! That way you get more out of your effort."

"O.K.," said Tom. Roger nodded. Again they braced themselves against the hatch.

"One—two—three—*push*!" counted Tom.

Slowly, applying the pressure evenly, they heaved against the steel hatch. Tom's head swam dizzily, as the blood raced through his veins.

"Keep going," gasped Astro. "I think it's giving a little!"

Tom and Roger pushed with the last ounce of strength in their bodies, and after a final desperate effort, slumped to the floor breathless. Astro continued to push, but a moment later, relaxed and slipped down beside Tom and Roger.

They sat on the deck for nearly five minutes gasping for air.

"Like—" began Roger, "like father—like son!" He blurted the words out bitterly.

"Like who?" asked Astro.

"Like my father," said Roger in a hard voice. He got up and walked unsteadily over to the oxygen bottle and kicked it. "Empty!" he said with a harsh laugh. "Empty and we only have one more bottle. Empty as my head the day I got into this space-happy outfit!"

"You going to start that again!" growled Astro. "I thought you had grown out of your childish bellyaching about the Academy." Astro eyed the blond cadet with a cold eye. "And now, just because you're in a tough spot, you start whining again!"

"Knock it off, Astro," snapped Tom. "Come on. Let's give this hatch another try. I think it gave a little on that last push."

"Never-say-die Corbett!" snarled Roger. "Let's give it the old try for dear old Space Academy!"

Tom whirled around and stood face to face with Manning.

"I think maybe Astro's right, Roger," he said coldly. "I think you're a foul ball, a space-gassing hot-shot that can't take it when the chips are down!"

"That's right," said Roger coldly. "I'm just what you say! Go ahead, push against that hatch until your insides drop out and see if you can open it!" He paused and looked directly at Tom. "If that sand has penetrated inside the ship far enough and heavily enough to jam that hatch, you can imagine what is on top, outside! A mountain of sand! And we're buried under it with about eight hours of oxygen left!"

Tom and Astro were silent, thinking about the truth in Roger's words. Roger walked slowly across the deck and stood in front of them defiantly.

"You were counting on the ship being spotted by Captain Strong or part of a supposed searching party! Ha! What makes you think three cadets are so important that the Solar Guard will take time out to look for us? And if they *do* come looking for us, the only thing left up there now"—he pointed his finger over his head—"is a pile of sand like any other sand dune on this crummy planet. We're stuck, Corbett, so lay off that last chance, do-or-die routine. I've been eating glory all my life. If I do have to splash in now, I want it to be on my own terms. And that's to just sit here and wait for it to come. And if they pin the Medal—the Solar Medal—on me, I'm going to be up there where all good spacemen go, having the last laugh, when they put my name alongside my father's!"

"Your father's?" asked Tom bewilderedly.

"Yeah, my father. Kenneth Rogers Manning, Captain in the Solar Guard. Graduate of Space Academy, class of 2329, killed while on duty in space, June 2335. Awarded the Solar Medal *posthumously*. Leaving a widow and one son, *me*!"

Astro and Tom looked at each other dumfounded.

"Surprised, huh?" Roger's voice grew bitter. "Maybe that clears up a few things for you. Like why I never missed on an exam. I never missed because I've lived with Academy textbooks since I was old enough to read. Or why I wanted the radar deck instead of the control deck. I didn't want to have to make a decision! My father had to make a decision once. As skipper and pilot of the ship he decided to save a crewman's life. He died saving a bum, a no good space-crawling rat!"

Tom and Astro sat stupefied at Roger's bitter tirade. He turned away from them and gave a short laugh.

"I've lived with only one idea in my head since I was big enough to know why other kids had fathers to play ball with them and I didn't. To get into the Academy, get the training and then get out and cash in! Other kids had fathers. All I had was a lousy hunk of gold, worth exactly five hundred credits! A Solar Medal. And my mother! Trying to scrape by on a lousy pension that was only enough to keep us going, but not enough to get me the extra things other kids had. It couldn't bring back my father!"

"That night—in Galaxy Hall, when you were crying—?" asked Tom.

"So eavesdropping is one of your talents too, eh, Corbett?" asked Roger sarcastically.

"Now, wait a minute, Roger," said Astro, getting up.

"Stay out of this, Astro!" snapped Roger. He paused and looked back at Tom. "Remember that night on the monorail going into Atom City? That man Bernard who bought dinner for us? He was a boyhood friend of my father's. He didn't recognize me, and I didn't tell him who I was because I didn't want you space creeps to know that much about me. And remember, when I gave Al James the brush in that restaurant in Atom City? He was talking about the old days, and he might have spilled the beans too. It all adds up, doesn't it? I had a reason I told you and it's just this! To make Space Academy pay me back! To train me to be one of the best astrogators in the universe so I could go into commercial ships and pile up credits! Plenty of credits and have a good life, and be sure my mother had a good life—what's left of it. And the whole thing goes right back to when my father made the decision to let a space rat live, and die in his place! So leave me alone with your last big efforts—and grandstand play for glory. From now on, keep your big fat mouth shut!"

"I—I don't know what to say, Roger," began Tom.

"Don't try to say anything, Tom," said Astro. There was a coldness in his voice that made Tom turn around and stare questioningly at the big Venusian.

"You can't answer him because you came from a good home. With a mom and pop and brother and sister. You had it good. You were lucky, but I don't hold it against you because you had a nice life and I didn't." Astro continued softly, "You can't answer Mr. Hot-shot Manning, but I can!"

"What do you mean?" asked Tom.

"I mean that Manning doesn't know what it is to really have it tough!"

"You got a *real* hard luck story, eh, big boy?" snarled Roger.

"Yeah, I have!" growled Astro. "I got one that'll make your life look like a spaceman's dream. At least you *know* about your father. And you lived with your mother. I didn't have *anything—nothing*! Did you hear that, Manning? I didn't even have a pair of shoes, until I found a kid at the Venusport spaceport one day and figured his shoes would fit me. I beat the space gas out of him and took his shoes. And then they were so tight, they hurt my feet. I don't know who my father was, nothing about him, except that he was a spaceman. A rocket buster, like me. And my mother? She died when I was born. Since I can remember, I've been on my own. When I was twelve, I was hanging around the spaceport day and night. I learned to buck rockets by going aboard when the ships were cradled for repairs, running dry runs, going through the motions, I talked to spacemen—all who would listen to me. I lied about my age, and because I was a big kid, I was blasting off when I was fifteen. What little education I've got, I picked up listening to the crew talk on long hops and listening to every audioslide I could get my hands on. I've had it tough. And because I *have* had it tough, I want to forget about it. I don't want to be reminded what it's like to be so hungry that I'd go out into jungles and trap small animals and take a chance on meeting a tyrannosaurus. So lay off that stuff about feeling sorry for yourself. And about Tom being a hero, because with all your space gas you still can't take it! And if you don't want to fight to live, then go lie down in the corner and just keep your big mouth shut!"

Tom stood staring at the big cadet. His head jutted forward from his shoulders, the veins in his neck standing out like thick cords. He knew Astro had been an orphan, but he had never suspected the big cadet's life had been anything like that which he had just described.

Roger had stood perfectly still while Astro spoke. Now, as the big cadet walked back to the hatch and nervously began to examine the edges with his finger tips, Roger walked over and stood behind him.

"Well, you knuckle-headed orphan," said Roger, "are you going to get us out of here, or not?"

Astro whirled around, his face grim, his hands balled into fists, ready to fight. "What's that, Mann—?" He stopped. Roger was smiling and holding out his hand.

"Whether you like it or not, you poor little waif, you've just made yourself a friend."

Tom came up to them and leaned against the door casually. "When you two stop gawking at each other like long-lost brothers," he said lazily, "suppose we try to figure a way out of this dungeon."

CHAPTER 19

"Tom—Roger!" shouted Astro. "I think I've got it!"

Astro, on his knees, pulled a long file blade away from the hatch and jumped to his feet.

"Did you cut all the way through?" asked Tom.

"I don't know—at least I'm not sure," Astro replied, looking down at the hole he had made in the hatch. "But let's give it a try!"

"Think we can force it back enough to get a good hold on it?" asked Roger.

"We'll know in a minute, Roger," said Astro. "Get that steel bar over there and I'll try to slip it in between the hatch and the bulkhead."

Roger rummaged around in the jumble of broken parts and tools on the opposite side of the power deck and found the steel bar Astro wanted. After several attempts to force the hatch open had proven futile, Tom suggested that they try to file the hinges off the hatch, and then attempt to slide it sideways. After much effort, and working in shifts, they had filed through the three hinges, and now were ready to make a last desperate attempt to escape. Astro took the steel bar from Roger and jammed it between the bulkhead wall and the hatch.

"No telling what we'll find on the other side," said Astro. "If the sand has covered up the ship all the way down to here, then we'll never get out!"

"Couldn't we tunnel through it to the top, if it has filled the ship down as far as here?" asked Roger.

"Not through this stuff," said Tom. "It's just like powder."

"Tom's right," said Astro. "As soon as you dig into it, it'll fall right back in on you." He paused and looked at the hatch thoughtfully. "No. The only way we can get out of here is if the sand was only blown into the deck outside and hasn't filled the rest of the ship."

"Only one way to find out," said Tom.

"Yeah," agreed Roger. "Let's get that hatch shoved aside and take a look."

Astro jammed the heavy steel bar farther into the space between the hatch and the bulkhead, and then turned back to his unit-mates.

"Get that piece of pipe over there," he said. "We'll slip it over the end of the bar and that'll give us more leverage."

Tom and Roger scrambled after the length of pipe, slipped it over the end of the bar, and then, holding it at either end, began to apply even pressure against the hatch.

Gradually, a half inch at a time, the heavy steel hatch began to move sideways, sliding out and behind the bulkhead. And as the opening grew larger the fine powderlike sand began to fall into the power deck.

"Let's move it back about a foot and a half," said Tom. "That'll give us plenty of room to get through and see what's on the other side."

Astro and Roger nodded in agreement.

Once more the three boys exerted their strength against the pipe and applied pressure to the hatch. Slowly, grudgingly it moved back, until there was an eighteen-inch opening, exposing a solid wall of the desert sand. Suddenly, as if released by a hidden switch, the sand began to pour into the power deck.

"Watch out!" shouted Tom. The three boys jumped back and looked on in dismay as the sand came rushing through the opening. Gradually it slowed to a stop and the pile in front of the opening rose as high as the hatch itself.

"That does it," said Tom. "Now we've got to dig through and find out how deep that stuff is. And spacemen, between you and me, I hope it doesn't prove too deep!"

"I've been thinking, Tom," said Roger, "suppose it's as high as the upper decks outside? All we have to do is keep digging it out and spreading it around the power deck here until we can get through."

"Only one thing wrong with that idea, Roger," said Tom. "If the whole upper part of the ship is flooded with that stuff, we won't have enough room to spread it around."

"We could always open the reaction chamber and fill that," suggested Astro, indicating the hatch in the floor of the power deck that lead to the reactant chamber.

"I'd just as soon take my chances with sand," said Roger, "as risk opening that hatch. The chamber is still hot from the wildcatting reaction mass we had to dump back in space."

"Well, then, let's start digging," said Tom. He picked up an empty grease bucket and began filling it with sand.

"You two get busy loading them, and I'll dump," said Astro.

"O.K.," replied Tom and continued digging into the sand with his hands.

"Here, use this, Tom," said Roger, offering an empty Martian water container.

Slowly, the three cadets worked their way through the pile on the deck in front of the hatch opening and then started on the main pile in the opening itself. But as soon as they made a little progress on the main pile, the sand would fall right in again from the open hatch, and after two hours of steady work, the sand in front of the hatch still filled the entire opening. Their work had been all for nothing. They sat down for a rest.

"Let's try it a little higher up, Tom," suggested Roger. "Maybe this stuff isn't as deep as we think."

Tom nodded and stepped up, feeling around the top of the opening. He began clawing at the sand overhead. The sand still came pouring through the opening.

"See anything?" asked Astro.

"I—don't—know—" spluttered Tom as the sand slid down burying him to his waist.

"Better back up, Tom," warned Roger. "Might be a cave-in and you'll get buried."

"Wait a minute!" shouted Tom. "I think I see something!"

"A light?" asked Astro eagerly.

"Careful, Tom," warned Roger again.

Tom clawed at the top of the pile, ignoring the sand that was heaped around him.

"I've got it," shouted Tom, struggling back into the power deck just in time to avoid being buried under a sudden avalanche. "There's another hatch up there, just behind the ladder that leads into the passenger lounge. That's the side facing the storm! And as soon as we dig a little, the sand falls from that pile. But the opposite side, leading to the jet-boat deck, is free and clear!"

"Then all we have to do is force our way through to the top," said Astro.

"That's all," said Tom. "We'd be here until doomsday digging our way clear."

"I get it!" said Roger. "The storm filled up the side of the ship facing that way, and that is where the passenger lounge is. I remember now. I left the hatch open when we came down here to the power deck, so the sand just kept pouring in." He smiled sheepishly. "I guess it's all my fault."

"Never mind that now!" said Tom. "Take this hose and stick it in your mouth, Astro. Breath through your mouth and plug up your nose so you won't get it all stopped up with sand while you pull your way through."

"I'll take this rope with me too," said Astro. "That way I can help pull you guys up after me."

"Good idea," said Roger.

"As soon as you get outside the hatch here," said Tom, "turn back this way. Keep your face up against the bulkhead until you get to the top. Right above you is the ladder. You can grab it to pull yourself up."

"O.K.," said Astro and took the length of hose and put it in his mouth. Then, taking a piece of waste cotton, he stopped up his nose and tested the hose.

"Can you breathe O.K.?" asked Tom.

Astro signaled that he could and stepped through the hatch. He turned, and facing backward, began clawing his way upward.

"Keep that hose clear, Roger!" ordered Tom. "There's about five feet of sand that he has to dig through and if any of it gets into the hose—well—"

"Don't worry, Tom," interrupted Roger. "I've got the end of the hose right next to the oxygen bottle. He's getting pure stuff!"

Soon the big cadet was lost to view. Only the slow movement of the hose and rope indicated that Astro was all right. Finally the hose and rope stopped moving.

Tom and Roger looked at each other, worried.

"You think something might be wrong?" asked Tom.

"I don't know—" Roger caught himself. "Say, look—the rope! It's jerking—Astro's signaling!"

"He made it!" cried Tom.

"I wonder if—" Roger suddenly picked up the end of the hose and spoke into it. "Astro? Hey, Astro, can you hear me?"

"Sure I can." Astro's voice came back through the hose. "Don't shout so loud! I'm not on Earth, you know. I'm just ten feet above you!"

Roger and Tom clapped each other on the shoulders in glee.

"All set down there?" called Astro, through the hose.

"O.K." replied Tom.

"Listen," said Astro, "when you get outside the hatch, you'll find a pipe running along the bulkhead right over your head. Grab that and pull yourself up. Tie the rope around your shoulder, but leave enough of it so the next guy can come up. We don't have any way of getting it back down there!" he warned. "Who's coming up first?"

Tom looked at Roger.

"You're stronger, Tom," said Roger. "You go up now and then you can give Astro a hand pulling me through."

"All right," agreed Tom. He began pulling the hose back through the sand. He took the end, cleared it out with a few blasts from the oxygen bottle and put it in his mouth. Then, after Roger had helped him tie the rope around his shoulders, he stuffed his nose with the waste cotton. He stepped to the opening. Roger gave three quick jerks on the rope and Astro started hauling in.

With Astro's help, Tom was soon free and clear, standing beside Astro on the jet-boat deck.

"Phoooeeeey!" said Tom, spitting out the sand that had filtered into his mouth. "I never want to do that again!" He dusted himself off and flashed his emergency light around the deck. "Look at that!" he said in amazement. "If we'd kept on digging, we'd have been trapped down there for—" he paused and looked at Astro who was grinning—"a long, long time!" He held the light on the sand that was flowing out of the open hatch of the passenger lounge.

"Come on," urged Astro. "Let's get Roger out of there!"

They called to Roger through the hose and told him to bring two more emergency lights and the remainder of the Martian water. Three minutes later the *Polaris* unit was together again.

Standing on the deck beside his two unit-mates, Roger brushed himself off and smiled. "Well," he said, "looks like we made it!"

"Yeah," said Tom, "but take a look at this!" He walked across the jet-boat deck to the nearest window port. What should have been a clear view of the desert was a mass of solidly packed sand.

"Oh, no!" cried Roger. "Don't tell me we have to go through that again?"

"I don't think it'll be so bad this time," said Astro.

"Why not?" asked Tom.

"The sand is banked the heaviest on the port side of the ship. And the window ports on the starboard side of the control deck were pretty high off the ground."

"Well, let's not just stand here and talk about it," said Roger. "Let's take a look!" He turned and walked through the jet-boat deck.

Tom and Astro followed the blond cadet through the darkened passages of the dead ship, and after digging a small pile of sand away from the control-deck hatch, found themselves once more amid the jumble of the wrecked instruments.

For the first time in three days, the boys saw sunlight streaking through the crystal port.

"I told you," cried Astro triumphantly.

"But there still isn't any way out of this place!" said Roger. "We can't break that port. It's six inches thick!"

"Find me a wrench," said Astro. "I can take the whole window port apart from inside. How do you think they replace these things when they get cracked?"

Hurriedly searching through the rubble, Tom finally produced a wrench and handed it to Astro. In a half hour Astro had taken the whole section down and had pushed the crystal outward. The air of the desert rushed into the control room in a hot blast.

"Whew!" cried Roger. "It must be at least a hundred and twenty-five degrees out there!"

"Come on. Let's take a look," said Tom. "And keep your fingers crossed!"

"Why?" asked Roger.

"That we can dig enough of the sand away from the ship to make it recognizable from the air."

Following Tom's lead, Roger and Astro climbed through the open port and out onto the sand.

"Well, blast my jets!" said Astro. "You can't even tell there was a storm."

"You can't if you don't look at the ship," said Tom bitterly. "That was the only thing around here of any size that would offer resistance to the sand and make it pile up. And, spaceman, look at that pile!"

Astro and Roger turned to look at the spaceship. Instead of seeing the ship, they saw a small mountain of sand, well over a hundred feet high. They walked around it and soon discovered that the window port in the control deck had been the only possible way out.

"Call it what you want," said Roger, "but I think it's just plain dumb luck that we were able to get out!" He eyed the mound of sand. Unless one knew there was a spaceship beneath it, it would have been impossible to distinguish it from the rest of the desert.

"We're not in the clear yet!" commented Astro grimly. "It would take a hundred men at least a week to clear away enough of that sand so search parties could recognize it." He glanced toward the horizon. "There isn't anything but sand here, fellows, sand that stretches for a thousand miles in every direction."

"And we've got to walk it," said Tom.

"Either that or sit here and die of thirst," said Roger.

"Any canals around here, Tom?" asked Astro softly.

"There better be," replied Tom thoughtfully. He turned to Roger. "If you can estimate our position, Roger, I'll go back inside and see if I can find a chart to plot it on. That way, we might get a direction to start on at least."

Astro glanced up at the pale-blue sky. "It's going to be a hot day," he said softly, looking out over the flat plain of the desert, "an awful hot day!"

CHAPTER 20

"Got everything we need?" asked Tom.

"Everything we'll need—and about all we can safely carry without weighing ourselves down too much," answered Roger. "Enough food for a week, the rest of the Martian water, space goggles to protect our eyes from the sun and emergency lights for each of us."

"Not much to walk a hundred and fifty miles on," offered Astro. "Too bad the sand got in the galley and messed up the rest of that good food."

"We'll have plenty to get us by—if my calculations are right," said Tom. "One hundred and fifty-four miles to be exact."

"*Exact* only as far as my sun sight told me," said Roger.

"Do you think it's right?" asked Tom.

"I'll answer you this way," Roger replied. "I took that sight six times in a half hour and got a mean average on all of them that came out within a few miles of each other. If I'm wrong, I'm very wrong, but if I'm right, we're within three to five miles of the position I gave you."

"That's good enough for me," said Astro. "If we're going out there"—he pointed toward the desert—"instead of sitting around here waiting for Strong or someone to show up, then I'd just as soon go now!"

"Wait a minute, fellas. Let's get this straight," said Tom. "We're all agreed that the odds on Captain Strong's showing up here before our water runs out are too great to risk it, and that we'll try to reach the nearest canal. The most important thing in this place is water. If we stay and the water we have runs out, we're done for. If we go, we might not reach the canal—and the chance of being spotted in the desert is even smaller than if we wait here at the ship." He paused. "So we move on?" He looked at the others. Astro nodded and looked at Roger, who bobbed his head in agreement.

"O.K., then," said Tom, "it's settled. We'll move at night when it's cool, and try to rest during the day when it's the hottest."

Roger looked up at the blazing white sphere in the pale-blue sky that burned down relentlessly. "I figure we have about six hours before she drops for the day," he said.

"Then let's go back inside the ship and get some rest," he said.

Without another word, the three cadets climbed back inside the ship and made places for themselves amid the littered deck of the control room. A hot wind blew out of the New Sahara through the open port like a breath of fire. Stripped to their shorts, the three boys lay around the deck unable to sleep, each thinking quietly about the task ahead, each remembering stories of the early pioneers who first reached Mars. In the mad rush for the uranium-yielding pitchblende, they had swarmed over the deserts toward the dwarf mountains by the thousands. Greedy, thinking only of the fortunes that could be torn from the rugged little mountains, they had come unprepared for the heat of the Martian deserts and nine out of ten had never returned.

Each boy thought, too, of the dangers they had just faced. This new danger was different. This was something that couldn't be defeated with an idea or a sudden lucky break. This danger was ever present—a fight against nature, man against the elements on an alien planet. It was a battle of endurance that would wring the last drop of moisture mercilessly from the body, until it became a dry, brittle husk.

"Getting pretty close to sundown," said Tom finally. He stood beside the open port and shielded his eyes from the glare of the sun, now slowly sinking below the Martian horizon.

"I guess we'd better get going," said Roger. "All set, Astro?"

"Ready, Roger," answered the Venusian.

The three boys dressed and arranged the food packs on their backs. Tom carried the remainder of the Martian water, two quart plastic containers, and a six-yard square of space cloth, an extremely durable flyweight fabric that would serve as protection from the sun during the rest stop of the day. Roger and Astro carried the food in compact packs on their backs. Each boy wore a makeshift hat of space cloth, along with space goggles, a clear sheet of colored plastic that fitted snugly across the face. All three carried emergency lights salvaged from the wrecked ship.

Tom walked out away from the ship several hundred yards and studied his pocket compass. He held it steady for a moment, watching the needle swing around. He turned and walked slowly still watching the needle of the compass. He waited for it to steady again, then turned back to Roger and Astro who stood watching from the window port.

"This is the way." Tom pointed away from the ship. "Three degrees south of east, one hundred and fifty-four miles away, if everything is correct, should bring us smack on top of a major canal."

"So long, *Lady Venus*," said Astro, as he left the ship.

"Don't think it hasn't been fun," added Roger, "because it hasn't!"

Astro fell in behind Roger, who in turn followed Tom who walked some ten feet ahead. A light breeze sprang up and blew across the surface of the powdery sand. Ten minutes later, when they stopped to adjust their shoulder packs, they looked back. The breeze had obliterated their tracks and the mountain of sand covering the spaceship appeared to be no different from any of the other small dunes on the desert. The New Sahara desert of Mars had claimed another Earth-ship victim.

"If we can't see the *Lady Venus* standing still, and knowing where to look," said Astro, "how could a man in a rocket scout ever find it?"

"He wouldn't," said Roger flatly. "And when the water ran out, we'd just be sitting there."

"We're losing time," said Tom. "Let's move." He lengthened his stride through the soft sand that sucked at his high space boots and faced the already dimming horizon. The light breeze felt good on his face.

* * * * *

The three cadets had no fear of running into anything in their march through the darkness across the shifting sands. And only an occasional flash of the emergency light to check the compass was necessary to keep them moving in the right direction.

There wasn't much talk. There wasn't much to talk about. About nine o'clock the boys stopped and opened one of the containers of food and ate a quick meal of sandwiches. This was followed by a carefully measured ounce of water, and fifteen minutes later they resumed their march across the New Sahara.

About ten o'clock, Deimos, one of the small twin moons of Mars, swung up overhead, washing the desert with a pale cold light. By morning, when the cherry-red sun broke the line of the horizon, Tom estimated that they had walked about twenty miles.

"Think we ought to camp here?" asked Astro.

"If you can show me a better spot," said Roger with a laugh, "I'll be happy to use it!" He swung his arm in a wide circle, indicating a wasteland of sand that spread as far as the eyes could see.

"I could go for another hour or so," said Astro, "before it gets too hot."

"And wait for the heat to reach the top of the thermometer? Uh-huh, not me," said Roger. "I'll take as much sleep as I can get now—while it's still a little cool."

"Roger's right," said Tom. "We'd better take it easy now. We won't be able to get much sleep after noon."

"What do we do from noon until evening?" asked Astro.

"Aside from just sitting under this hunk of space cloth, I guess we'll come as close to being roasted alive as a human can get."

"You want to eat now?" asked Astro.

Tom and Roger laughed. "I'm not hungry, but you go ahead," said Tom. "I know that appetite of yours won't wait."

"I'm not too hungry either," said Roger. "Go ahead, you clobber-headed juice jockey."

Astro grinned sheepishly, and opening one of the containers of food, quickly wolfed down a breakfast of smoked Venusian fatfish.

Tom and Roger began spreading the space cloth on the sand that was already hot to the touch. Anchoring the four corners in the sand with the emergency lights and one of Tom's boots, they propped up the center with the food packs, one on top of the other. A crude tent was the result and both boys crawled in under, sprawling on the sand. Astro finished eating, lay down beside his two unit-mates, and in a moment the three cadets were sound asleep.

The sun climbed steadily over the desert while the *Polaris* unit slept. With each hour, the heat of the desert rose, climbing past the hundred mark, reaching one hundred and twenty, then one hundred and thirty-five degrees.

Tom woke up with a start. He felt as if he were inside a blazing furnace. He rolled over and saw Astro and Roger still asleep, sweat pouring off them in small rivulets. He started to wake them, but decided against it and just lay still under the thin sheet of space cloth that protected him from the sun. As light as the fabric square was, weighing no more than a pound, under the intense heat of the sun it felt like a woolen blanket where it touched him. Astro rolled over and opened his eyes.

"What time is it, Tom?"

"Must be about noon. How do you feel?"

"I'm not sure yet. I had a dream." The big cadet rubbed his eyes and wiped the sweat from his forehead. "I dreamed I was being shoved into an oven—like Hansel and Gretel in that old fairy tale."

"Personally," mumbled Roger, without opening his eyes, "I'll take Hansel and Gretel. They might be a little more tender."

"I could do with a drink," said Astro, looking at Tom.

Tom hesitated. He felt that as hot as it was, it would get still hotter and there had to be strict control of the remainder of the water.

"Try to hold out a little longer, Astro," said Tom. "This heat hasn't really begun yet. You could drink the whole thing and still want more."

"That's right, Astro," said Roger, sitting up. "Best thing to do is just wet your tongue and lips a little. Drinking won't do much good now."

"O.K. by me," said Astro. "Well, what do we do now?"

"We sit here and we wait," answered Tom. He sat up and held the space cloth up on his side.

"You get in the middle, Astro," suggested Roger. "Your head is up higher than mine and Tom's. You can be the tent pole under this big top."

Astro grunted and changed places with the smaller cadet.

"Think there might be a breeze if we opened up one side of this thing?" asked Roger.

"If there was a breeze," answered Tom, "it'd be so hot, it'd be worse than what we've got inside."

"It sure is going to be a hot day," said Astro softly.

The thin fabric of the space cloth was enough to protect them from the direct rays of the sun, but offered very little protection against the heat. Soon the inside of the tent was boiling under the relentless sun.

They sat far apart, their knees pulled up, heads bowed. Once when the heat seemed unbearable, Tom opened one side of the cloth in a desperate hope that it might be a little cooler outside. A blast of hot air entered the makeshift tent and he quickly closed the opening.

About three o'clock Roger suddenly slipped backward and lay sprawled on the sand.

Tom opened one of the containers of water and dipped his shirttail into it. Astro watched him moisten Roger's lips and wipe his temples. In a few moments the cadet stirred and opened his eyes.

"I—I—don't know what happened," he said slowly. "Everything started swimming and then went black."

"You fainted," said Tom simply.

"What time is it?" asked Astro.

"Sun should be dropping soon now, in another couple of hours."

They were silent again. The sun continued its journey across the sky and at last began to slip behind the horizon. When the last red rays stretched across the sandy desert, the three cadets folded back the space-cloth covering and stood up. A soft evening breeze sprang up, refreshing them a little, and though none of them was hungry, each boy ate a light meal.

Tom opened the container of water again and measured out about an ounce apiece.

"Moisten your tongue, and sip it slowly," ordered Tom.

Roger and Astro took their share of the water and dipped fingers in it, wiping their lips and eyelids. They continued to do this until finally, no longer able to resist, they took the precious water and swished it around in their mouths before swallowing it.

They folded the space cloth, shouldered their packs, and after Tom had checked the compass, started their long march toward their plotted destination.

They had survived their first twenty-four hours in the barren wastes of the New Sahara, with each boy acutely aware that there was at least a week more of the same in front of them. The sky blackened, and soon after Deimos rose and started climbing across the dark sky.

CHAPTER 21

"How much water left?" asked Astro thickly.

"Enough for one more drink apiece," Tom replied.

"And then what happens?" mumbled Roger through his cracked lips.

"You know what will happen, Roger—you know and I know and Tom knows," muttered Astro grimly.

For eight days they had been struggling across the blistering shifting sands, walking by night, sweltering under the thin space cloth during the day. Their tongues were swollen. Scraggly beards covered their chins and jaws. Roger's lips were cracked. The back of Tom's neck had suffered ten minutes of direct sun and turned into a large swollen blister. Only Astro appeared to be bearing up under the ordeal. There was no sign of their being close to the canal.

"Wanta try marching during the day?" asked Astro. They had broken camp on the evening of the eighth day and were preparing to move on into the never-changing desert.

"If we don't hit the canal sometime during the night, there might be a chance it's close enough to reach in a couple of hours," replied Tom. "Either that, or we've miscalculated altogether."

"How about you, Roger?" asked Astro.

"Whatever you guys decide, I'll be right in back of you." Roger had grown steadily weaker during the last three days and found it difficult to sleep during the hours of rest.

"Then we'll keep marching tomorrow," said Astro.

"Let's move out," said Tom. Roger and Astro shouldered the remaining slender food packs, with Tom carrying the water and space cloth, and they started out into the rapidly darkening desert.

Once again, as on the previous eight nights, the little moon, Deimos, swung across the sky, casting dim shadows ahead of the three marching boys. Tom found it necessary to look at the compass more often. He couldn't trust his sense of direction as much as he had earlier. Once, he had gone for two hours in a direction that was fifty degrees off course. The rest stops also were more frequent now, with each boy throwing his pack to the ground and lying flat on his back, to enjoy the cool breeze that never failed to soothe their scorched faces.

When the sun rose out of the desert on the morning of the ninth day, they stopped, ate a light breakfast of preserved figs, divided the juice evenly among them, and, ripping the space cloth into three sections, wrapped it around themselves like Arabs and continued to walk.

By noon, with the sun directly overhead, they were staggering. At two-thirty the sun and the heat were so overpowering that they stopped involuntarily and tried to sit on the hot sand only to find that they couldn't and so they stumbled on.

Neither Roger nor Astro asked for water. Finally Tom stopped and faced his two unit-mates wobbling on unsteady legs.

"I've gone as far as I can without water. I—I don't think I can go another step. So come on, we'll finish what we've got."

Astro and Roger nodded in quiet agreement. They watched with dull eyes as Tom carefully opened the plastic container of water. He gave each a cup and slowly, cautiously, measured out the remaining water into three equal parts. He held the container up for a full minute allowing the last drop to run out before tossing the empty bottle to one side.

"Here goes," said Tom. He wet his lips, placed a wet finger on his temples and sipped the liquid slowly, allowing it to trickle down his parched throat.

Roger and Astro did the same. After he had wet his lips, Astro took the full amount in his mouth and washed it around, before swallowing it. Roger brought the cup up slowly to his mouth with trembling hands, tipped it shakily, and then before Astro or Tom could catch him, fell to the ground. The precious water spilled into the sand.

Tom and Astro watched dumfounded as the dry sand sucked away the water until nothing remained but a damp spot six inches wide.

"I guess—" began Tom, "I guess that about does it!"

"We'll have to carry him," said Astro simply.

Tom looked up into the eyes of his unit-mate. There he saw a determination that would not be defeated. He nodded his head and stooped over to grapple with Roger's legs. He got one leg under each arm and then tried to straighten up. He fell to the sand and rolled to one side. Astro watched him get up slowly, wearily, his space-cloth covering remaining on the ground, and then, with gritted teeth, try once more to pick Roger's legs up.

Astro put out his hand and touched Tom on the shoulder. His voice was low, hardly above a whisper. "You lead the way, Tom. I'll carry him."

"You lead the way, Tom. I'll carry him."

Tom looked up at the big Venusian. Their eyes locked for a moment and then he nodded his head and turned away. He pulled out the pocket compass and through blurred vision read the course beneath its wavering needle. He waved an arm in a direction to the right of them and staggered off.

Astro stooped down, picked Roger up in his arms and slowly got him across his shoulders. Then steadying himself, he walked after Tom.

Suddenly a blast of wind, hot as fire, swept across the sandy plains, whipping the sand up and around the two walking figures, biting into exposed hands and faces. Tom tried to adjust his goggles when the sand began to penetrate around the edges but his fingers shook and he dropped them. In a flash, the sand drove into his eyes, blinding him.

"I can't see, Astro," said Tom in a hoarse whisper when Astro staggered up. "You'll have to guide."

Astro took the compass out of Tom's hand and then placed his unit-mate's hand on his back. Tom gripped the loose folds of the space cloth and uniform beneath and struggled blindly after the big cadet.

The hot sun bore down. The wind kept blowing and Astro, with Roger slung across his back like a sack of potatoes and Tom clinging blindly to his uniform, walked steadily on.

He felt each step would be his last, but with each step he told himself through gritted teeth that he could do ten more—and then ten more—ten more.

He walked, he staggered, and once he fell to the ground, Tom slumping behind him and Roger being tossed limply to the scorching sand. Slowly Astro recovered, helped Tom to his feet, then with the last of his great strength, picked up Roger again. This time, he was unable to get him to his shoulder so he carried him like a baby in his arms.

At last the sun began to drop in the red sky. Astro felt Roger's limp body slipping from his grip. By now, Tom had lost all but the very last ounce of his strength and was simply being pulled along.

"Tom—" gasped Astro with great effort, "I'm going to count to a thousand and then—I'm going to stop."

Tom didn't answer.

Astro began to count. "One—two—three—four—five—six—" He tried to make each number become a step forward. He closed his eyes. It wasn't important which way he went. It was only important that he walk those thousand steps, "five hundred eleven—five hundred twelve—five hundred thirteen—"

Involuntarily he opened his eyes when he felt himself climbing up a small rise in the sand. He opened his eyes and ten feet away was the flat blue surface of the canal they had been searching for.

"You can let go now, Tom," said Astro in a voice hardly above a whisper. "We made it. We're on the bank of the canal."

* * * * *

"Hey, Roger," yelled Astro from the middle of the canal, "ever see a guy make like a submarine?"

Tom and Roger sat on the top of the low bank of the canal drying off from a swim, while Astro still splashed around luxuriating in the cool water.

"Go on," yelled Roger, "let's see you drown yourself!"

"Not me, hot-shot," yelled Astro. "After that walk, all I'd have to do is open my mouth and start drinking."

Finally tiring of his sport, the big Venusian pulled himself up onto the bank of the canal and quickly dressed. Pulling on his space boots, he turned to Tom and Roger, who were breaking out the last two containers of food.

"You know, Astro," said Roger quietly, "I'll never be able to repay you for carrying me."

Tom was quiet for a moment, and then added, "Same here, Astro."

Astro grinned from ear to ear. "Answer me this one question, both of you. Would you have done it for me?"

The two boys nodded.

"Then you paid me. As long as I know I'm backed up by two guys like you, then I'm paid. Carrying you, Roger, was just something I could do for you at that particular time. One of these days, when we get out of this oven, there'll come a time when you or Tom will do something for me—and that's the way it should be."

"Thanks, Astro," said Roger. He reached over and put his hand on top of Astro's, and then Tom placed his hand on top of theirs. The three boys were quiet for a moment. There was an understanding in each of them that they had accomplished more than just survival in a desert. They had learned to respect each other. They were a unit at last.

"What do we do next?" asked Roger.

"Start walking that way," said Tom, pointing to his left along the bank of the canal that stretched off in a straight line to the very horizon. "If we're lucky, we might be able to find something to use as a raft and then we can ride."

"Think there are any fish in this canal?" asked Astro, gazing out over the cool blue water.

"Doubt it. At least I've never heard of there being any," replied Tom.

"Well," said Roger, standing up, "you can go a lot farther without food than you can without water. And we still have that big container of ham left."

"Yeah, as soon as it gets hot, we just swim instead of walk," said Astro. "And, believe me, there's going to be a lot of swimming done!"

"Think we might strike anything down that way," asked Roger. He looked down the canal in the direction Tom had indicated.

"That's the direction of the nearest atmosphere booster station. At least that was the way it looked on the chart. All of them were built near the canals."

"How far away do you think it is?" asked Astro.

"Must be at least three hundred miles."

"Let's start moving," said Roger, "and hope we can find something that'll float us on the canal."

Single file, wearing the space cloths once more as protection against the sun, they walked along the bank of the canal. When the heat became unbearable, they dipped the squares of space cloths into the water and wrapped themselves in them. When they began to dry out, they would repeat the process. At noon, when the sun dried the fabric nearly as fast as they could wet it, they stopped and slipped over the edge of the bank into the cool water. Covering their heads with the cloths they remained partly submerged until the late afternoon. When the sun had lost some of its power, again they climbed out and continued walking.

Marching late into the night, they made camp beside the canal, finished the last container of food, and, for the first time since leaving the ship, slept during the night. By the time Deimos had risen in the sky, they were sound asleep.

CHAPTER 22

"Eeeeeeoooooooow!" Astro's bull-like roar shattered the silence of the desert. "There—up ahead, Tom—Roger—a building!"

Tom and Roger stopped and strained their eyes in the bright sunshine.

"I think you're right," said Tom at last. "But I doubt if anyone's there. Looks like an abandoned mining shack to me."

"Who wants to stand here and debate the question?" asked Roger, and started off down the side of the canal at a lope, with Astro and Tom right behind him.

During the last three days the boys had been living off the contents of the last remaining food container and the few lichens they found growing along the canal. Their strength was weakening, but with an abundant supply of water near at hand and able to combat the sun's heat with frequent swims, they were still in fair condition.

Tom was the first to reach the building, a one-story structure made of dried mud from the canal. The shutters and the door had long since been torn away by countless sandstorms.

The three boys entered the one-room building cautiously. The floor was covered with sand, and sand was piled in heaping drifts in front of the open windows and door.

"Nothing—not a thing," said Roger disgustedly. "This place must be at least a hundred and fifty years old."

"Probably built by a miner," commented Tom.

"What do you mean 'nothing'?" said Astro. "Look!"

They followed Astro's pointing finger to the ceiling. Crisscrossed, from wall to wall, were heavy wooden beams.

"Raft!" Tom cried.

"That's right, spaceman," said Astro, "a raft. There's enough wood up there to float the *Polaris*. Come on!"

Astro hurried outside, with Tom and Roger following at his heels. They quickly climbed to the roof of the old building and soon were ripping the beams from the crumbling mud. Fortunately the beams had been joined by notching the ends of the crosspieces. Astro explained that this was necessary because of the premium on nails when the house was built. Everything at that time had to be hauled from Earth, and no one wanted to pay the price heavy nails and bolts demanded.

One by one, they removed the heavy beams, until they had eight of them lined up alongside the edge of the canal.

"How do we keep them together?" asked Roger.

"With this!" said Tom. He began ripping his space cloth into long strips. Astro and Roger tugged at the first beam. At last they had it in the water.

"It floats," cried Astro. Tom and Roger couldn't help but shout for joy. They quickly hauled the remaining beams into the water and lashed them together. Without hesitation, they shoved the raft into the canal, climbing aboard and standing like conquering heroes, as the raft moved out into the main flow of the canal and began to drift forward.

"I dub thee—*Polaris the Second*," said Tom in formal tones and gave the nearest beam a kick.

Astro and Roger gave a lusty cheer.

Steadily, silently, the raft bore them through the never-changing scene of the canal's muddy banks and the endlessness of the desert beyond.

Protecting themselves from the sun during the day by repeated dunkings in the water, they traveled day and night in a straight course down the center of the canal. At night, the tiny moon, Deimos, climbed across the desert and reflected light upon the satin-smooth water.

The third day on the raft they began to feel the pangs of hunger. And where during their march through the desert, their thoughts were of water, now visions of endless tables of food occupied their thoughts. At first, they talked of their hunger, dreaming up wild combinations of dishes and giving even wilder estimates of how much each could consume. Finally, discovering that talking about it only intensified their desire, they kept a stolid silence. When the heat became unbearable, they simply took to the water. Once Tom's grip on the raft slipped and Roger plunged in after him without a moment's hesitation, only to have Astro go in to save both of them.

On and on—down the canal, the three boys floated. Days turned into nights, and nights, cooling and refreshing, gave way to the blazing sun of the next day. The silent desert swept past them.

One night, when Astro, unable to sleep, was staring ahead into the darkness, he heard a rustling in the water alongside the raft. He moved slowly to the edge of the raft and peered down into the clear water.

He saw a fish!

The big cadet watched it dart around the raft. He waited, his body tense. Once the fish came to the edge of the raft, but before Astro could move his arm, it darted off in another direction.

At last the fish disappeared and Astro sank back on the timbers. He trailed one hand over the side in the water, and suddenly, felt the rough scales of the fish brush his fingers. In a flash, Astro closed his hand and snatched the wriggling creature out of the water.

"Tom—Roger—" he shouted. "Look—look—a fish—I caught a fish with my bare hands!"

Tom rolled over and opened his eyes. Roger sat in bewilderment.

"I watched him—I was watching him and then he went away. And then I held my hand over the side of the raft and he came snooping around and—well, I just grabbed him!"

He held the fish in the viselike grip of his right hand until it stopped moving.

"You know," said Tom weakly, "I just remembered. When we were in the Science Building in Atom City, one of their projects was to breed both Earth and Venus fish in the canals."

"I am going to shake, personally, the hand of the man who started this project when we get back to Atom City," said Astro.

Suddenly Roger gripped Tom's arms. He was staring in the direction the raft was going. "Tom—" he breathed, "Astro— look!"

They turned and peered into the dusk. In the distance, not a mile away, was the huge crystal-clear dome of the atmosphere booster station, its roaring atomic motors sending a steady purring sound out across the desert.

"We made it," said Tom, choking back the tears. "We made it!"

"Well, blast my jets," said Astro. "We sure did!"

* * * * *

"And you mean to tell me, you *walked* across that desert?" asked Captain Strong.

Tom glanced over at Astro and Roger. "We sure did, sir."

"With Astro doing the last stretch to the canal carrying me and dragging Tom," said Roger as he sipped his hot broth.

The room in the chief engineer's quarters at the atmosphere station was crowded with workers, enlisted Solar Guardsmen and officers of the Solar Guard. They stood around staring in disbelief at the three disheveled cadets.

"But how did you ever survive?" asked Strong. "By the craters of Luna, that blasted desert was hotter this past month than it has ever been since Mars was first colonized by Earthmen. Why—why—you were walking through temperatures that reached a hundred and fifty degrees!"

"You don't have to convince us, sir," said Roger with a smile. "We'll never forget it as long as we live."

Later, when Tom, Roger and Astro had taken a shower and dressed in fresh uniforms, Strong came in with an audioscriber and the three cadets gave the full version of their adventure for the official report back to the Academy. When they had finished, Strong told them of his efforts to find them.

"We knew you were in trouble right away," said Strong, "and we tracked you on radar. But that blasted storm fouled us all up. We figured that the sand would have covered up the ship, and that the chances of finding you in a scout were very small, so I got permission from Commander Walters to organize this ground search for you." He paused. "Frankly we had just about given up hope. Took us three weeks finally to locate the section of desert you landed in."

"We knew you would come, sir," said Tom, "but we didn't have enough water to wait for you—and we had to leave."

"Boys," said Strong slowly, "I've had a lot of wonderful things happen to me in the Solar Guard. But I have to confess that seeing you three space-brained idiots clinging to that raft, ready to eat a raw fish—well, that was just about the happiest moment of my life."

"Thank you, sir," said Roger, "and I think I can speak for Tom and Astro when I say that seeing you here with over a hundred men, and all this equipment, ready to start searching for us in that desert—well, it makes us feel pretty proud to be members of an outfit where the skipper feels that way about his crew!"

"What happens now, sir?" asked Tom.

"Aside from getting a well-deserved liberty, it's back to the old grind at the Academy. The *Polaris* is at the spaceport at Marsopolis, waiting for us." He paused and eyed the three cadets with a smile. "I guess the routine at Space Academy will seem a little dull now, after what you've been through."

"Captain Strong," said Astro formally, "I *know* I speak for Tom and Roger when I say that *routine* is all we want for a long time to come!"

"Amen!" added Tom and Roger in unison.

"Very well," said Strong. "*Polaris* unit—Staaaaand *TO!*"

The three boys snapped to attention.

"You are hereby ordered to report aboard the *Polaris* at fifteen hundred hours and stand by to raise ship!"

He returned their salutes, turned sharply and walked from the room.

Outside, Steve Strong leaned against the wall and stared through the crystal shell of the atmosphere station into the endless desert.

"Thank you, Mars," he said softly, "for making spacemen out of the *Polaris* crew!" He saluted sharply and walked away.

Tom suddenly burst from the room with Roger and Astro yelling after him.

"Hey, Tom, where you going?" yelled Roger.

"I've got to get a bottle of that water out of the canal for my kid brother Billy!" shouted Tom and disappeared down a slidestairs.

Roger turned to Astro and said, "That's what I call a real spaceman."

"What do you mean?" asked Astro.

"After what we've been through, he still remembers that his kid brother wants a bottle of water from a canal as a souvenir!"

"Yeah," breathed Astro, "Tom Corbett is—is—a real spaceman!"

BIBLIOBAZAAR

The essential book market!

Did you know that you can get any of our titles in large print?

Did you know that we have an ever-growing collection of books in many languages?

Order online:
www.bibliobazaar.com

Find all of your favorite classic books!

Stay up to date with the latest government reports!

At BiblioBazaar, we aim to make knowledge more accessible by making thousands of titles available to you- *quickly and affordably*.

Contact us:
BiblioBazaar
PO Box 21206
Charleston, SC 29413

LaVergne, TN USA
10 December 2009
166621LV00001B/12/A